A DEA

Zach wanted some time to himself, to think. He grinned and waved to Lou as as she flitted out with the other ladies, then he ambled to the rear of the mansion and stepped out into the muggy night. Under a canopy of stars the estate lay quiet. Restless, he walked to a tall weeping willow and leaned against the trunk.

Off in the darkness something moved. Zach spied a figure in the shadows and thought it might be a servant. "Who's there?" he asked.

The answer came in the form of dully glittering steel as a dagger flashed out of the gloom, streaking directly at Zach's heart.

WILDERNESS
Blood Kin

David Thompson

LEISURE BOOKS NEW YORK CITY

To Judy, Joshua, and Shane

A LEISURE BOOK®

August 2000

Published by

Dorchester Publishing Co., Inc.
276 Fifth Avenue
New York, NY 10001

ISBN 0-8439-4757-8

The name "Leisure Books" and the stylized "L" with design are trademarks of Dorchester Publishing Co., Inc.

Printed in the United States of America.

Blood Kin

Chapter One

"It's your deal, Injun. Make sure you keep the cards on top of the table where we can see 'em."

The thinly veiled insult caused Zachary King to tense. For a moment he considered leaping across the table and throttling the man responsible. But then he glanced at Adam Tyler, who sat on his right, and remembered what Tyler had told him the previous night: "The first rule of gambling, son, is to never let your emotions get the better of you. You do and you're dead. It's as simple as that."

Swallowing his pride, Zach picked up the deck and shuffled as Adam had taught him. When he dealt, he did so slowly, deliberately, so everyone could plainly see he was dealing from the top.

"Hell, Injun," said the same player who had insulted him before. "A damn turtle could go faster than you."

Adam Tyler cleared his throat. He was a tall, broad-

7

shouldered man, dressed in an expensive black suit and frilled white shirt. His brown hair, greying at the temples, was neatly combed. Gray-blue eyes that glinted like steel blades fixed on the speaker. "Is it something you ate, Brak? Is that why you're so disagreeable tonight? Or is it that you just don't like the cut of my young friend's clothes?"

Zach didn't quite understand Tyler's last remark. His clothes were as fine as the gambler's. In fact, Tyler had given them to him. They consisted of a double-breasted blue frock coat, striped trousers, a tartan vest, shirt and silk cravat. Typical attire for white men in St. Louis, Zach had learned. His long raven hair was tucked under his jacket, which was open at the front so he had quick access to his pistols and bowie.

The man called Brak paused in the act of reaching for his cards. He was a beefy chunk of muscle with beetling brows and dark, beady eyes. His brown suit was the best money could buy but it was rumpled and wrinkled, as if he had slept in it, and flecked with specks of dust and food. "He's your friend, you say? Adopting wayward pups now, are you, Tyler?"

"My personal business, Brak, is none of your concern." A sharp edge laced the tall gambler's casual comment.

"And I would never presume to pry," Brak responded. "I'm surprised, is all. You've always been a loner." Brak fixed his beady eyes on Zach. "Though, now that I think of it, I did hear someone mention you had taken a kid under your wing. Of course, I never figured it would be a half-breed."

Zach tensed again. Being called a 'breed never sat well with him. All his life he'd had to put up with bigoted whites and red men alike who looked down their noses at him because of his mixed lineage. He'd had no say in who his parents were, yet most held it against him, as if having a white father and a Shoshone mother somehow made him inferior. "I'd rather you didn't call me that," he said harshly.

Brak grinned. "A mite touchy, are we? Sure, kid. What-ever you want. I'm happy to oblige a friend of Tyler's." Picking up his cards, he shot a barb at the tall gambler. "Your protégé has a lot to learn, doesn't he?"

Adam Tyler frowned—and so did Zach. He was upset at himself for letting the gambler down. His only excuse was that he was new to the game. He'd only developed a passion for it in the past couple of days. So, yes, he would be the first to admit he had a lot to learn. But he wanted to acquit himself proudly, if for no other reason than to prove to Adam that he was worthy of the gambler's time and instruction.

Tyler suddenly pushed a pile of chips to the center of the table. "I open at two hundred, gentlemen."

The other two players glanced at one another. Brak blinked, then began counting his own chips. "Isn't that a little steep? The usual amount has been twenty."

"I have a good hand," Tyler said. "If you want to see exactly *how* good, put up or shut up."

Brak leaned back, his thick brows knitting. "Now I've heard everything. The great Adam Tyler bragging about his cards? Before anyone else has even bet? Only a beginner like this 'breed would be so foolish. What are you up to, Tyler?"

"It will cost you three hundred to find out."

"A challenge? Is that what this is?" Brak laughed coldly. "Very well. I'll see your three hundred and raise you an-other fifty."

Zach laid down his cards. He had come into the game with thirty dollars to his name and was another thirty ahead. He intended to *stay* ahead, too, in order to prove to Louisa that wagering at cards could be profitable. The other two players also folded, leaving Tyler and the troublemaker.

"I'll see you," the former said and held up a single finger.

Zach dealt Tyler a card. Brak requested two. The stakes rose to four hundred and twenty dollars. At last the moment

9

of truth came, and Brak, smirking, laid down a straight, all hearts.

"Beat that, if you can."

Adam Tyler showed his hand one card at a time. In a neat row he lined up four Kings and the two of diamonds, then raked in the pot. "I thank you, gentlemen, for an evening's diversion. Now my young friend and I must excuse ourselves."

Brak wasn't pleased. "You're leaving without giving us a chance to win our money back? That's hardly sporting."

"Poker is a game of chance, not a charity," Tyler said. "After all these years you still have a lot to learn, don't you?"

Having his own question thrown in his face angered Brak, but he tried hard not to show it. "Another time, then, Tyler. Bring the pup along. I might as well fleece the both of you as one. And think of what it will do for my reputation."

Tyler rose and slipped his wallet into an inner pocket. "We're all well aware of your reputation," he stated with a smile. Yet he somehow contrived to make it the most insulting remark of all. Taking his wide-brimmed black hat from a peg on the wall, he said, "Come along, Zachary. We shouldn't keep your fiancée waiting."

They waded through dense clouds of cigar and cigarette smoke and out the grand double doors of The Golden Bough. Tyler adjusted his hat while striding down the steps. "You did well in there, son. You controlled your temper admirably."

It was past eleven at night yet carriages and pedestrians bustled by in a steady stream. After a week in St. Lous, Zach still couldn't get over how many people there were and how they never seemed to sleep. "You don't think much of Brak, do you?"

"I don't think much of anyone who divides the human race into sheep and those who shear them." Tyler turned left. "You'll find, son, that there are two types of gamblers in this world. Greedy men like Phil Brak, who are out to take every sucker for all they can, and those who see gambling as an honorable profession."

"As you do," Zach said. One of the reasons he liked Adam Tyler so much was Tyler's strong sense of personal honor. It reminded him greatly of his pa.

"I like to think of gambling as jousting with cards," Tyler said, smiling. "Blame it on my mother. When I was young she liked to read Walter Scott's *Ivanhoe* to me, and ever since I've tried to live like a chivalrous knight in shining armor. Only in my case, it's a frock coat."

"My pa liked to read to us when we were little, too," Zach revealed. Most whites east of the Mississippi tended to think of trappers and mountain men as uncouth, illiterate simpletons who couldn't read or write, but the truth was that nearly every mountaineer Zach ever met could do both. Many were quite fond of books, which they devoured by the dozens during the long winters months when twenty foot snowdrifts confined them to their cabins or lodges for days on end. The mountain men even had a special nickname for it, the Rocky Mountain College.

Some had a special passion for great literary works like *Ivanhoe*. Zach knew of two, Jim Bridger and Shakespeare McNair, who were extremely fond of the Bard of Avon and would spend hours around a campfire reciting his works for the benefit of their companions.

Zach always liked to listen to his father read, but he had never been much of a reader himself. He preferred to be out doing things rather than sitting around indoors with a book in hand. His pa claimed he was missing out on a lot, that books taught important lessons well worth learning. But the way Zach saw it, anything he could learn from a book he could also learn from real life.

Zach became aware that Adam Tyler was talking to him.

"—met a lot of men like Brak in my profession. You'll meet them, too. When you do, as the old saying goes, grin and bear it."

11

"I don't intend to gamble forever," Zach said, realizing his newfound mentor assumed he meant to do just that. It was a pleasant way to pass the time until Lou's kinfolk showed up, was all.

"Why not? I can tell you like the game. You have a natural talent, and you could go far."

"You're serious?" Zach had to admit he liked the challenge and excitement, but he had never considered making a living at it. In a month or so Louisa and him were bound for the Rockies where they already had a pristine valley all picked out for their homestead. It had a year-round stream, plenty of grass for grazing, woodland that harbored abundant game, and best of all, it was only a two-day ride from his folks' place.

"Very serious." Tyler clapped Zach on the back. "Give it some thought. I can teach you all you need to know. You might never become rich but you'll always be able to afford to keep a roof over your head and food on the table."

"Me? A gambler?" Zach couldn't get over the notion. It was silly. And yet—and yet he *did* enjoy raking in a wining pot and the look on the faces of the men he beat. In a limited way, it was similar to counting coup. Only it was done with playing cards instead of a coup stick or a war club.

"Why not?" Tyler asked. "Because of who you are? No matter what line of work you pick, there will always be bigots like Brak who can't see past the color of your skin. For that matter, many people don't think all that highly of the gambling fraternity. You'll be doubly despised."

"Just what I need," Zach quipped, wondering what his betrothed would say about the idea.

Louisa May Clark was dreaming. In it, she and Zachary were in a stately white church with a high steeple. The seats were crammed with well-wishers, and her uncle was escorting her down the carpeted aisle toward the altar and Zach. A beautiful wedding dress clung to her slim form, a thin veil hung over her eyes. She couldn't stop smiling, for this was the single most happiest event of her life. She was about to wed the man she loved.

Then a strange thing happened.

Lou was halfway down the aisle when the happy features of the onlookers changed. Their faces became masks of feral hatred. They sneered at her, cursed her, shouting things like, " 'Breed lover!" and "Squaw woman!" She asked them to stop but they yelled louder, all of them pointing accusingly, some spitting on her. Tears welled up and Lou pleaded for them to desist but they either didn't hear her or didn't care.

From out of their midst came a familiar figure. "How could you, Louisa? How could you betray me like this?"

"Pa?" Lou couldn't credit her eyes. Her father was dead, slain by hostiles. He couldn't be at her wedding. He just couldn't.

"He's not good enough for you, little one. You should marry above your station, not below it. I didn't raise you just so you could throw your life away on a romantic lark."

Lou began to bawl. Her father had never talked to her like that before. So far as she knew, there wasn't a lick of prejudice in his bones. "I love Zach!" she cried. "I love him with all my heart and soul!"

"Do you?" her pa asked. His query was echoed by every member of the congregation. Over and over again they chanted accusingly, "Do you? Do you? Do you? Do you?"

With the chant echoing in her head, Lou abruptly awakened and snapped bolt upright. It took a minute for it to sink in where she was, in a bed in the spare bedroom at Adam Tyler's house. She was caked with perspiration and trembling as if cold. A block of ice encased her heart. Or was it a block of fear? she fretted as she slid to the edge and stood.

The lantern was lit. In its rosy light Lou saw her reflection in the mirror attached to the door. She had on a plain but pretty dress, bought that morning at a local shop. Zach had said she could have any one she wanted, but they were trying to make their money last as long as possible so she'd settled for the cheapest available.

Which explained why she had been so annoyed, earlier, when Zach announced he was taking most of what they had left to go gamble. She'd about thrown a fit until Adam Tyler assured her he would watch out for Zach. And, the truth be told, they needed more money. Their stay in St. Louis was being extended. Not by choice, since they were both eager to return to the mountains. No, her relatives were to blame.

They were missing.

Lou couldn't begin to imagine what had happened.

How vividly she recollected the day a rider showed up at the King cabin and dropped off a letter from her Aunt Martha. In it, Martha wrote that she, her husband and son, would be in St. Louis for the entire month of August, waiting to meet with Lou and her father, Zebulon. One of Zeb's brothers, along with his two daughters, would also be there.

None of them knew Lou's pa was dead. She'd never written them, never felt the need. Lou had Zach and Zach's family. Nate and Winona King had taken her into their home and made her as much a part of their family as Zach and their little girl, Evelyn. Lou had never been happier, never more content, never felt more at peace with the world.

Her aunt's letter, though, sparked feelings Lou had long denied. Martha and the others were blood kin. She's spent many an hour perched on Martha's knee when she was little, many a day and week in the company of her cousins. Lou owed it to them, she felt, to go meet them in person to tell about her father.

Then, too, Lou couldn't wait to impart the good news about her engagement. Zach was the best thing to ever happen to her, and she couldn't wait to share her happiness with her kinfolk. She figured her aunt and uncles and cousins would be delighted.

Which made Lou's dream all the more mystifying. Aunt Martha had been one of those in the pews. Her cousins Harry, Ethel, and Gladys had been there, also, pointing and chanting along with the rest. What was she to make of it all?

Shaking her head, Lou opened the door and walked down the hall to the sitting room. Tyler's home was nicely furnished, with thick beige carpeting, dusky drapes, and polished mahogany furniture. It was comfortable yet undeniably masculine. A rumbling noise, like the snort of a boar, drew her gaze to the divan.

Stretched out flat on his back was the gambler's other houseguest, an old, grizzled trapper Zach had befriended. George Milhouse had been a free trapper once but nowadays he ran a shop devoted to the trapping trade. A spry, feisty veteran of years in the high country, he sported a mane of white hair and needed a hickory cane to get around. At the moment he was sound asleep and snoring loud enough to be heard in Blackfoot country.

Lou, grinning impishly, crept to the divan and bent down. Lightly applying her thumb and forefinger to the oldster's nose, she gently squeezed. Milhouse was still for a few seconds, then he sputtered, bucked, and came up off the divan as if his buckskins were on fire. Lou laughed with glee.

"What in tarnation?" Milhouse thundered, looking around in confusion. Divining that she had played a trick on him, he snatched his cane from off the floor and swung it at her backside but didn't connect. "Another of your deviltries, girl? I swear, you're worse than a ten-year-old. That feller of yours ought to check none of his brains have oozed out his ears before he ties the knot."

"That's not nice," Lou chided.

"Neither is scarin' a fragile old man half to death," Milhouse said, running a hand through his hair.

Lou moved toward the kitchen. "Fragile, my foot. You're

15

about as delicate as a grizzly. I hope Zach has half your energy when he's your age."

George Milhouse chuckled. "Flattery, child, will get you everywhere. How about you treat me to a cup of coffee and maybe I'll see fit to forgive you."

"Maybe?" Lou taunted. The stove was warm, some embers from suppertime smoldering. A few puffs, and Lou had them red hot. From a bin by the kitchen counter, she selected several logs and shoved them in.

Milhouse took a seat at the table, setting his cane on top. "You know, missy, if I were forty years younger I'd be next in line behind Zach. You're the kind of woman a man would never get bored with."

"I thank you, kind sir," Lou said, performing a curtsy.

"See what I mean? You're a regular bundle of surprises. None of my wives were half as much fun as you. My first one, a white gal, was a born nag. My second, a Crow, was lazier than me. The third, a Flathead, wouldn't so much as let me spit in our lodge or she'd bean me with a rock. And my fourth, a Bannock, was forever giving me sass. About wore out my ears, that woman did."

Lou sat across from him. She was so accustomed to wearing buckskins up in the mountains that she had to remind herself to cross her legs and sit as ladies were expected to sit. It wouldn't do for her to roost with her legs wide apart in front of Aunt Martha, who was a stickler for proper behavior. "You must have had some fun with them."

"Oh, we had our share of laughs, sure enough," Milhouse said. "But none were very playful. Maybe that's because they were older than you are."

"I'm seventeen," Lou reminded him. By that age most girls were married. Anyone not wed by, say, twenty-two, was branded a spinster.

"Gettin' on in years, are you?" the old trapper said and laughed uproariously. "Hellfire, girl. You're still a sprout. As green as grass behind the ears but too proud to admit it." Milhouse sighed. "I envy you, though. You and that young hardhead of yours."

"Zach is eighteen, and he's every inch the man you are," Lou said. More so, in her estimation. To her, Zachary King—or Stalking Coyote, as he was known among the Shoshones—was the handsomest, sweetest, kindest, most special man alive. Being near him did things to her, provoked feelings and thoughts no other man ever had. She craved him with every fiber of her being, as if he were a part of her she couldn't do without.

Milhouse winked. "I wouldn't be so sure, missy. None of my wives had any complaints." Slapping his thigh, he cackled again.

"My, my, you're certainly in a good mood."

"Why shouldn't I be? We've got that Festerman business taken care of. You're safe, my shop hasn't been burned to the ground, and none of us were killed. What more can a body ask for?"

Lou conceded his point. Lon Festerman had been one of the richest, most powerful men in all of St. Louis. He'd also been a vile monster, a purveyor of lust and debauchery who had kidnaped her and planned to force her into a life of prostitution. Her darling Zach, with the help of Adam Tyler and Milhouse, had thwarted Festerman's plan, killing Festerman in the process. She had a lot to be thankful for. Still, she was worried. "I'd be a lot happier if I knew what happened to my relatives. They're not at the hotel they're supposed to be at."

"Didn't they leave a message?"

"No." Lou and Zach had gone to the Grand Imperial Hotel down by the levee but the clerk had told them her aunt and the rest checked out about a week ago. The clerk had no idea where they had gone. "It's not like my Aunt Martha. She wouldn't run off without leaving word."

Milhouse scratched his stubbly chin. "Could be she didn't leave one because she hadn't heard from you. Didn't you say you just up and headed for St. Louis after gettin'

17

her letter? How was she to know you were on your way?"

Again the mountaineer had a point. "Even so, she should have left word." Now Lou had no idea where to look. Canvassing every hotel would take days. Add in all the inns and homes where travelers might stay, and it would require weeks of steady searching to find them. If they were even still in the city.

"Tell me again about these kinfolk of yours. How many are there, exactly?"

"Six. There's my Aunt Martha, who is my mother's older sister, and her husband, Earnest, a lawyer. Plus their son, Harry, who works in a mill."

"Strange place for a lawyer's son to work," Milhouse commented.

"Harry was never the brightest of boys." Lou was being charitable. Poor Harry had been teased to no end when he was younger because his brains weren't equal to his brawn. Earnest was severely disappointed that Harry wasn't bright enough to pass the bar, but to his credit Earnest never badgered the boy about it as Aunt Martha often did.

"And the others?" Milhouse prompted.

"Oh. They would be my father's brother, Uncle Thomas, and his two daughters, Ethel and Gladys. They were my best friends when I was little. We went everywhere and did everything together. I can't wait to see them."

"I hope they're as tickled to see you."

"Why wouldn't they be?" Lou shifted toward the stove. Steam was rising from the pot's spout, but it would be a while yet before the coffee was adequately brewed.

"When we're sprouts, sometimes we don't see the world as it really is or the people in it as they truly are."

"What are you trying to say? They're my relatives. Blood kin. I loved them all dearly as a child, and I still do. I can't wait to hear how they're doing and to share the news of my engagement. They'll be so happy for me."

Milhouse was about to say something when his glance shifted past her. He froze, his eyes widening in surprise.

Suddenly rising, he moved as briskly as he was able to the back door and yanked it open.

Startled, Louisa rose and followed. He had stopped on the threshold and was scanning the backyard, his cane held in front of him as if it were a sword. "What in the world has gotten into you?" she asked.

"Hush!" Milhouse said and went farther. "Did you hear that?"

Lou hadn't heard a thing. She stepped out into the muggy darkness. The humidity was much worse than up in the mountains and took some getting used to. Overhead, stars sparkled. Oddly, she'd noticed that fewer were visible in St. Louis than in high country. Perhaps the altitude was to blame. Or maybe the lights of the city had something to do with it.

"Someone just went over the back fence and down the alley." Milhouse turned to the small window to the left of the door. "He was peekin' in at us and hightailed it when I spotted him."

"Maybe you imagined it." Lou couldn't see anyone going around peering into windows at that time of night. They were liable to be shot.

"I may be old," Milhouse said archly, "but I'm not deaf, dumb, and blind. I tell you, I saw some feller watchin' us. He had a face like a hawk's, with a hooked nose and evil eyes."

Lou giggled and folded her arms. "Did he have long, pointed ears and fangs, too? Now I know it was all in your head."

"Sassy wench," the old trapper grumbled. "You're too cocky for your own good. One of these days it will spell trouble. Mark my words, missy."

"Come inside. The coffee should be about done." Lou backed indoors. "I'll pull the curtains so our Peeping Tom won't bother us." She did just that, then went to the stove.

George Milhouse lingered in the doorway, sniffing the air like a bloodhound trying to catch a scent. "Make light of me all you want. But I don't like it. I don't like it one bit. I've got a bad feeling, like that time up in the Tetons when I saw an Indian up in the rocks, and the next thing our trapping party knew, Bloods jumped us."

Lou opened the cupboard and removed two cups. "There are no Bloods in St. Louis. Honestly, men can be so silly. We have nothing to worry about."

"I hope you're right," Milhouse said. Closing the door, he bolted it and said again, almost to himself, "I sure as blazes hope you're right."

Chapter Two

Zachary King and Adam Tyler were walking south on Hanover Street. They had just passed an alley that flanked the row of limestone residences where Tyler lived when Zach's keen eyes detected movement. "Hold up," he said quietly. Crouching, he verified that a shadowy figure was running in the opposite direction.

"What in the world are you doing?" the tall gambler asked.

"Silhouettes always stand out better when you're down low." Zach quoted his pa. "Someone just jumped over your back fence and is running off."

Tyler never questioned Zach's judgment. Without delay he headed into the alley, saying, "We've got to follow him, son. I've made more than a few enemies in my career. Let's find out who it is and what they're up to."

Zach had no objections. The thrill of the chase appealed

21

to him. Life in a big city, he'd discovered, was pathetically dull compared to life in the wilderness. Back in the mountains he could go hunting or exploring or on a raid with a Shoshone war party. In St. Louis there wasn't a pastime worth his interest other than gambling.

Zach glided in front of the gambler, hunched low so he could see the fleeing figure more clearly. Tyler imitated him. As they passed the fence Zach swore he heard the back door to Tyler's house close and muffled voices. One sounded like Louisa's. Automatically, Zach's pulse quickened. He contemplated going to check on her. But she sounded all right, and he wasn't about to desert Tyler when the man needed him, not after all Tyler had done for them. If not for the suave gambler, they'd never have saved Louisa from Lon Festerman. Zach was forever in Tyler's debt.

At the end of the alley was Oak Street. The figure turned left, moving at a brisk walk. He didn't bother to glance back. Evidently he had no idea he was being pursued.

Zach slowed at the corner and looked before stepping into the open. Now the figure was a block off, passing under a street lamp. Its bright glare highlighted a high silk hat and a flowing cloak.

"It's not a common footpad," Tyler whispered, referring to the roving thieves who infested the city after dark. "Not dressed like that."

"Maybe it's a friend of yours," Zach suggested.

"My friends come to the front door. They don't skulk around like an assassin." Tyler broke into a jog. "Two blocks from here there are carriages for hire. We mustn't let him reach them."

"I can catch him with no problem," Zach said. To demonstrate, he ran flat out, bounding like an antelope, his lithe muscles rippling under his clothes like those of a tawny cougar. It felt good to put his body to the test again, to feel the breeze on his face and the rising excitement of knowing that soon he would overtake their quarry.

The man heard him. Swiveling, the prowler took one look and bolted, moving amazingly quick for a city dweller, his cloak flowing behind him like a sheet in the wind.

"Damn." Zach increased his speed. He was confident he would overtake the man. Among the Shoshones he was considered fleet of foot. He couldn't beat his pa yet, but he'd won many a footrace against Shoshone youths his own age and older. Willing his legs to pump faster, he began to gain.

The man ran as if his heels were aflame. Several times he glanced back, and once Zach glimpsed a bony, angular face dominated by a large hooked nose.

They flew across an intersection and under stately maples. Up ahead were more street lamps lining a broad avenue, and parked along it were half a dozen carriages awaiting fares. A couple was getting into the first carriage in line, a middle-aged man and a woman half his age whose red dress clung to her like a second skin. Her bosom jutted like twin melons, about to explode through the garment.

"Zach! Don't tangle with him alone!" Adam Tyler hollered. He had fallen a score of yards behind and was doing his utmost not to lose any more ground.

Zach wasn't worried. He relished the prospect of a fight. A true Shoshone warrior lived for one purpose: to defeat his enemies in battle. It was in the heat of combat that coup was counted, and Zach's goal was to one day count more than any Shoshone ever had, to become war chief of the entire tribe.

As Zach narrowed the gap and drew within pouncing distance, he grinned in keen anticipation. He hoped the man would resist and give him an excuse to resort to his flintlocks or the bowie.

The avenue was a stone's throw away when the cloaked figure unexpectedly halted and whirled. Balling both fists, he crouched, adopting an odd stance with one leg out straight and the other bent at the knee.

Zach's grin widened. The dolt was making it almost too

easy. He rushed in, not bothering to draw a weapon, relying on his momentum to bowl the man over. But much to his astonishment the prowler evaded him with ease, pivoted, and landed a kick to Zach's back that sent Zach to his knees, his body lanced with pain.

In a twinkling Zach was on his feet again but the man was ready for him, still in that unusual stance. Zach threw a punch that would have dropped most anyone in St. Louis, but the figure in the cloak sidestepped and retaliated with another kick, this time to the thigh. Zach's entire leg went numb and was on the verge of buckling.

The man flicked a high kick that Zach blocked. He also countered a spinning foot strike to the groin. Then he aimed a kick of his own that missed by a mile. His adversary possessed uncanny reflexes, some of the best Zach ever witnessed. Zach drove a punch at his foe's jaw, again missing as the figure skipped sideways.

Adam Tyler arrived. He didn't follow Zach's example and engage the man one-on-one or try to talk the fellow into giving up. Instead, his right arm snapped up like a whip and a nickel-plated derringer materialized in his hand as if out of thin air. "That will be quite enough," he declared.

The hawk-faced prowler didn't agree. His right foot flashed, his instep connecting with the gambler's wrist. The derringer went flying.

In a pantherish bound the man was past them and crossing to the carriages. Zach started to limp after him, but Adam Tyler put a restraining hand on his shoulder.

"Let him go, son."

"Not on your life!" Zach would rather lose a limb than be bested. The humiliation would eat at him like a canker sore. No warrior worthy of the name would stand for it.

"There's no need," Tyler insisted.

Zach shrugged free but it was too late. The man in the cloak had reached the first carriage. The next moment the driver cracked his whip and it clattered into motion. "We can still catch him!"

"Weren't you listening? I recognized him. His name is Racine." Tyler turned to a strip of grass and bent down. "Did you see where my derringer fell?"

"No. Is this Racine an enemy of yours?"

"Not to my knowledge. He's a manservant, indentured to Jacques Goujon. Ah, here it is." Tyler retrieved the small gun, wiping it clean on his sleeve. "The Goujon family has lived in St. Louis since the French controlled it."

Zach was somewhat familiar with the city's checkered history. Originally a trading post started by two French fur traders, the settlement had later fallen under Spanish rule. The famous Louisiana Purchase resulted in the city becoming part of the United States, and since then it had grown by leaps and bounds, becoming the thriving gateway to the frontier.

"They're one of the oldest, wealthiest, and most respected families in the entire city," Tyler had gone on. "I've played cards on occasion with the eldest son, Auguste. There has never been ill-will between us."

"What could Racine have been up to?"

The gambler hiked his sleeve, exposing the clip that held the ivory-handled derringer in place. It consisted of a small metal plate designed to slide along his forearm on two thin round braces or rails. All Tyler had to do was flick his wrist and the derringer would shoot up his sleeve into his palm. "I'll find out tomorrow when I pay the Goujon family a visit."

"We'll find out, you mean," Zach amended.

"This doesn't concern you, son."

"My leg still hurts from where Racine kicked it. I'd say it most definitely does concern me." Zach rubbed the sore spot. "I've never seen anyone fight like he does, using his feet so much, with all those fancy spins."

"It's called savate," Tyler said. "*La boxe Francaise,* I believe the French call it. I saw Racine use it on another man once, a drunk who rudely accosted Jacques Goujon's daughter, Celeste. The drunk pulled a knife but he never

25

stood a prayer. Racine gave him a brutal, bloody beating."

"Savate?" Every day new facets of the white man's society were added to Zach's store of knowledge. Just when he thought he knew all there was to learn, along came something else.

"From what I understand the sport got its start in Paris about twenty years ago. Savate became so popular, clubs devoted to teaching it sprang up. A lot like the fencing clubs we have in New Orleans."

"And the bowie clubs?" Zach mentioned. He'd passed one just the other day. Jim Bowie, as everyone knew, had been a living legend. His exploits had been written up in all the papers, and his fabled weapon became so popular that knife makers sold them by the thousands. It was estimated that up to a third of the knives on the frontier now were bowie knives.

Jim Bowie's death at the Alamo—along with Davy Crockett, another living legend—had shocked the entire nation. Even Zach had been saddened to hear it. Bowie had been one of the few white men Zach truly admired. Fearless, daring, a bold adventurer and excellent fighter, Jim Bowie had all the traits Zach valued most, the traits every Shoshone warrior should have.

"Yes," Tyler said. He started to head back and Zach fell into step beside him. "But the bowie clubs aren't held in as high regard by the rich and privileged as the fencing and savate clubs are."

"Why is that?"

"Snobbery, plain and simple. The wealthy have a habit of thinking their money makes them special. They think they're a class apart from the common rabble." Tyler sighed. "Fencing has always been a sport of the aristocracy. Savate enjoys the same status. But the bowie clubs admit anyone and everyone who can pay the modest fee. It's the common man's sport, if you will. So the rich rarely indulge."

"Are there any savate clubs in St. Louis?"

"Just one. It opened up about a year ago. The instructor is a good friend of Jacques Goujon's, from what I hear."

"Have you ever gone to it?"

"I have no interest. Years ago I did take fencing lessons, though." Tyler patted his right sleeve. "But this is what I rely on to defend myself. It's never failed me yet."

"Until Racine kicked it out of your hand," Zach observed.

Tyler patted his other sleeve and grinned. "Why do you think I sometimes carry two?"

"Then you could have shot him if you wanted. Why didn't you?"

"Because he wasn't trying to hurt us, son. He was only protecting himself. Once we were no threat to him, he ran off rather than press his advantage. I suppose I could have put a ball into him as he was running to the carriage, but I've never shot anyone in the back and I never will."

The incident gave Zach much to ponder. He'd been toying with the idea of going to one of the bowie clubs to see if there was anything they could teach him that he didn't already know. Now he wondered if it might not be wiser to visit the savate club. It was a skill well worth learning, a skill that would make him a better warrior than he already was.

There was only one hitch. From what Tyler said, the lessons were expensive. Zach and Lou only had about seventy dollars to their name, and it had to last them for a month or more.

Zach had never given much thought to money before. Up in the mountains there was no need. They had little use for it.

Certainly not for food. In the Rockies game of all sorts was abundant. Deer, elk, buffalo, squirrels, rabbits, bear, mountain sheep, and countless other creatures thrived. When the King family needed something for the supper pot, all Zach had to do was walk out the cabin door, pick a target, and pull the trigger.

Certainly not for water, either. Theirs came from a large lake less than an arrow's flight away, a lake brimming with waterfowl and filled with fish. Toting buckets was a chore, but the water was sparkling clear and pure.

Clothing? Buckskins were their usual attire, fashioned from the hides of the deer they shot. Elk hides were used for rugs.

Nor did they need money for lodging. The log cabin they lived in hadn't cost them a penny. Even the valley in which it was located had been theirs for the taking.

The only time Zach's family ever spent money was for items nature's bounty couldn't provide. Items like beaver traps and fire steels and knives and guns and ammunition and black powder. Occasionally they indulged in luxuries, such as the glass panes his mother had wanted in their windows and curtains his mother had taken a shine to and a few personal articles. Small wonder, then, money had never been high on Zach's list of priorities.

Early on in life, however, Zach had learned that most white men valued it above all else, which had always amused him greatly. He'd thought it typical of them to value something so worthless.

Now Zach was having second thoughts. He's seen the sad look in Louisa's eyes when she had to put back a dress she liked and buy a cheaper one instead. For the first time since they'd met, he'd felt inadequate, as if he weren't doing his part in helping provide their wants and needs. The savate business bore the point home even more. He'd like to take lessons but they couldn't afford it.

"I'd like to meet the man who invented it," Zach griped.

"Invented what?" Adam Tyler responded.

"Oh, nothing," Zach said. "I was thinking out loud." An idea came to him. "Can we play poker again tomorrow night? And every night after? If I can win thirty dollars or more each time, by the end of the month Lou and I will have several hundred dollars."

The gambler smiled knowingly. "It doesn't quite work that way, my friend."

"What doesn't?"

"Winning. There are no guarantees. Sometimes the cards are in your favor, other times they're not. We call it playing hot or playing cold. Professionals never push their luck by playing when the cards the cold."

"So maybe I won't win quite as much. I'll still come out ahead," Zach said. "Besides, didn't you tell me that gambling is luck more than anything else? Some people have it, some don't, you said. I happen to have it."

"You do, do you?"

"I met Louisa, didn't I?" Zach figured that was proof in itself. They came from such totally different backgrounds and had grown up worlds apart, yet fate conspired to bring the two of them together against all odds. To his way of thinking it showed he was uncommonly lucky.

"She's your lucky charm, is she?" When Tyler saw Zach's puzzled expression, he elaborated. "Gamblers, by and large, are a superstitious lot. Some have good-luck charms they won't play without. It might be a ring, a rabbit's foot, anything. One fellow I knew carried the skull of a mouse around in a tiny pouch, believe it or not. The mouse had been a pet of his, and he used to keep it in his pocket when he played. For luck. Well, it died, so he kept the skull in the same pocket he'd kept the mouse. He honestly believed he'd lose without it."

"That's ridiculous."

"You'd think so, wouldn't you? Yet if it helps them play better, then having a good luck piece is worthwhile."

"You really think it does?"

Tyler grew thoughtful. "I've made a sort of personal study over the years, and I've noticed that when a player has a lucky charm they tend to be more relaxed and confident. So yes, I do."

A question occurred to Zach. "Do you have a lucky piece?"

The gambler grinned self-consciously. "Actually, yes. But if I show it to you, you must promise never to tell another living soul."

"You have my word."

Halting, Tyler reached into a pocket and brought out a small leather wallet which he carefully opened. Sliding his finger into a recessed compartment, he pulled out a folded strip of white cloth, faded with age. He held the cloth close to his chest and unfolded it, revealing a lock of golden hair. "This was Mary's. I cut it off the night she died in my arms. I never go anywhere without it."

Zach knew the story. How as a youth Tyler had been in love with a neighbor's daughter. The pair had planned to elope. But her father, who disapproved, sent men to kill Tyler, and in the conflict Mary was accidentally slain. She was the great love of Adam Tyler's life; he had never loved another, not in more than thirty years. "You believe her hair brings you luck?"

"Not so much that as peace of mind." Tyler tenderly stroked the golden strands, deep sorrow lining his face. "It's as if part of her is always with me."

Zach made bold to say, "I know it's none of my business, but she died such a long time ago. Why haven't you taken up with someone else by now?"

Tyler coughed, folded the cloth, and replaced the wallet. When he looked up, he wore a pained expression. "Don't you think I've tried? I've met other women who were attracted to me. But I never felt the same spark. Mary and I were meant for each other. We were two halves of the same coin. Our souls were linked, as she liked to say. I'll never find another like her. And at this stage, I don't much care to bother looking." Pausing, Tyler took a deep breath and squared his shoulders. "I'll go to my grave loving her. God willing, she and I will be reunited in the afterlife. If not, if there is no heaven or hell, if this life is all we have, then I'll die knowing I was true to her to the end."

Tremendous sympathy flooded through Zach. He imagined how he would feel if he was to lose Louisa, and he put his hand on the older man's wrist. "I'm sorry for you, Adam. I truly am."

Tyler's eyes misted. He coughed again, gave a toss of his head, and said, "It's not a subject I prefer to discuss. But I thank you, Zachary King, from the bottom of my heart. You're a good friend."

Zach was startled when the older man unexpectedly hugged him. Then they were walking again, neither saying a word, each lost in their own thoughts. They turned right on Juniper Street and were soon entering the limestone at 1420. Voices drew them to the kitchen where Louisa and George Milhouse were drinking coffee.

"Zach!" Lou squealed, overjoyed. Bounding from her chair, she threw herself into his arms and nuzzled his neck, forgetting they weren't alone.

Zach saw Milhouse smirk and felt himself blush. He couldn't help it. Showing deep affection was difficult enough. Doing so in front of others was downright embarrassing. Pecking Lou's cheek, he pried himself loose but left his arm draped around her slender waist. The smooth feel of her dress tingled his palm. Getting used to the sight of her in anything but buckskins took some doing, yet he had to admit she was spectacularly beautiful.

"So, how'd it go, young coon?" the old trapper inquired. "You're still wearing your shirt, so I reckon you came out a little ahead."

"A little," Zach conceded, then whispered how much in Lou's ear.

Louisa was ecstatic. Another thirty dollars meant they could stay in St. Louis an extra two weeks, possibly longer. "You must be quite the gambler," she complemented him and stifled a snicker when his chest expanded.

"I did all right."

Adam Tyler was pouring himself a cup of coffee. "He did better than all right. Your fiancé has potential, my dear.

Great potential. You might give some thought to letting him gamble regularly."

"He can do what he wants," Lou responded. "I have no say in the matter."

George Milhouse pealed with mirth. "Aren't you a caution, girl! That shows how much you know about bears and honey. To him, you're the queen of England and Cleopatra all rolled into one. You've got him so wrapped around your little finger, he won't hardly breathe without your say-so."

"That's silly," Lou said.

"Is it? Remember how he asked you five times if it was fine by you if he went with Adam tonight? Five times! Hellfire, before you know it, he'll be asking your permission to visit the outhouse."

Tyler, bursting into laughter, snorted coffee out his nose and had to put down the cup or risk spilling it.

Zach didn't say a thing. He'd learned the hard way that matching wits with the mountaineer was a hazardous proposition. Milhouse's body was decrepit but his mind was razor sharp.

"Honestly, Mr. Milhouse," Lou scolded. "Shouldn't you be telling them about the face at the window instead of poking fun at Zach and me?"

Adam Tyler instantly sobered. "What face?"

Lou explained, with the old trapper adding pertinent details where necessary. When she finished their host related the encounter he and Zach had with the same individual, leading Milhouse to beam at her and declare, "See? I told you so."

"Why was this man spying on us?" Lou asked.

"We'll know tomorrow," Tyler said, with a side glance at Zach. "Until then, I wouldn't fret. Racine is gone and I doubt very much he'll return. Everyone can get a good night's sleep."

Louisa clasped Zach's hand and said softly, "Care to tuck me in?" She knew it was a mistake when George Milhouse chortled. The man never missed an opportunity to tease them.

"Don't forget to undo his leash before you turn in. The poor boy might trip over it if he gets up in the middle of the night."

"You, sir, are impossible," Lou playfully huffed.

"You know, girlie, that's what all four of my wives claimed. Yet not one was willin' to swap me for another fella."

"I would have," was Lou's triumphant parting shot. Giggling, she led Zach down the hall to the spare bedroom. Tyler only had the one, which was granted to her by virtue of her gender. Zach slept out in the living room with Milhouse.

There had been a few awkward moments when the sleeping arrangements were initially discussed. Adam Tyler had hemmed and hawed, aware they weren't married and not knowing if they expected to stay together. Lou had set him straight. As much as she loved Zach—and she cared for him with all her heart and soul—they weren't going to take *that* step until *after* they were husband and wife.

Not that Louisa hadn't been tempted. Lord, how she'd wanted to share herself with him, totally, fully, in raw abandon! On the long ride across the prairie, sleeping at his side night after night, it had taken every ounce of willpower she possessed to keep her hands off him. Oh, they'd fooled around some, and once or twice she'd come awful close to losing her virginity. But always, at the brink of red-hot passion, they were able to pull back, to take deep breaths, and calm down. One time, though, much to her amusement, Zach had to jump in a stream, he was so aroused.

Now, in front of the bedroom door, Lou kissed him full on the mouth and even went so far as to rim his teeth with her tongue. She felt his muscular body harden, felt the hunger in his touch, saw it in his smoldering eyes. "I can't wait, my darling, until we're wed," she said huskily.

David Thompson

Nor could Zach. It was all he had dreamed of, all he had longed for, for months now. Lon Festerman had tried to spoil that dream and had paid with his life. The same would befall anyone who stood in their way. Anyone at all.

Chapter Three

St. Louis was a city of contrasts. Having been under French, Spanish, and now American control, it bore the stamp of each succeeding culture in its architecture, in the clothes the people wore, and in the people themselves. There was no common language. French, Spanish, and English were all used to more or less equal degrees, although since the United States assumed ownership English was gradually becoming the language of choice.

As for the city itself, the levee district by the river was the rowdiest, bawdiest, and most dangerous. Here the riverboats docked, dozens daily. It was the undisputed domain of the rivermen, the lusty, brawling, often vicious breed employed on the riverboats or at loading and unloading the millions of dollars in cargo filtered through the city yearly. The waterfront teemed with taverns, grog shops, and warehouses; "hell on earth" the locals called it, where no one was safe after dark.

Above the levee existed a different world, the pulsing heart of the growing metropolis. New arrivals were surprised to learn St. Louis boasted three newspapers, a bookstore, and two theaters. The city prided itself on its culture, on its magnificent tall buildings, on its many imposing places of worship with their sky-high steeples.

Situated around the central district, like spokes on a wheel, were other, mainly residential areas. In some, certain types of architecture were more predominant than elsewhere. In one, French-style homes were the rule. In another, classical Spanish construction prevailed. Then there were the Bostons, as they were dubbed, wealthy Americans who constructed mansions according to their personal specifications, resulting in residences that defied architectural stereotyping.

Even farther out were stately plantations. Jacques Goujon owned one such estate. His home was lavish in the extreme, yet not as ostentatious as those of his American counterparts. A winding gravel drive linked a wrought-iron gate to the mansion proper. Beyond were over a dozen outbuildings, among them a stable, a saw mill, and a wood shed.

Great wealth never failed to dazzle Zachary King. It was a whole new world to him, as alien in its way as the Shoshones would be to most whites. As their carriage rattled up the gravel drive, he gazed out the windows at the rows of leafy elms lining both sides. Everything about the estate bore the stamp of cultivation and refinement.

Louisa was gazing into the distance, at dark figures working in the fields. They were stooped over, doing exactly what, she couldn't say. She felt sorry for them, having to work in the heat of a summer's day. She saw a man on horseback moving among them, perhaps the overseer.

"Remember," Adam Tyler said. "Allow me to do most of the talking. We don't want to antagonize them without cause."

"I'd say being kicked by their manservant is cause enough," Zach mentioned.

"Racine is just one of many servants Goujon has. But diplomacy is called for, not violence. I'm sure Goujon will explain. He is an eminently reasonable man."

George Milhouse snickered. "It's the reasonable ones you've got to watch. They're usually holding a dagger behind their back in one hand while they offer to shake with the other."

Tyler looked at the oldster. "There was no need for you to come along, you know."

"Afraid my tongue will get us in hot water?" Milhouse laughed. "I might be gettin' on in years but I'm not senile. Don't worry. I know how to behave in public. I won't pee on the carpet, won't blow my nose on the drapes, or spit tobacco juice all over their fine linen. Happy?"

Louisa grinned. The gambler and the trapper had gone around and around about whether Milhouse should accompany them. Tyler had been dead set against it, but Milhouse wasn't to be denied. "I have to look out for my little angel," was how he'd put it, referring, of course, to her.

Lou adjusted her dress, praying she would be presentable. The rich and powerful were well outside her normal social circle. Butterflies fluttered in her stomach as the carriage began to roll to a stop in front of broad marble stairs. A grand portico fronted the mansion, which had been freshly repainted recently. "Isn't it marvelous?" she said to no one in particular.

Once again Zach felt a gnawing sense of failure as a potential provider. He would never have guessed Lou was so fond of money and the trappings that went with it. Worry blossomed. He couldn't see her settling for a small cabin up in the mountains after a visit to a place like this. "It's not so great," he said defensively.

"I've never seen a lovelier house," Lou said, mesmerized by its size and beauty.

"It's a mansion, dearie, not a plain old house," Geroge

Milhouse corrected her. "We wouldn't want you to offend our hosts. Poor Adam might have a cow."

A manservant in a brown suit and crisp white shirt descended to greet them. He had close-cropped hair and the same angular, swarthy features as Racine, Zach noted, commenting as much.

"He's a Cajun," Tyler said. "Many of Goujon's indentured servants are."

Zach made a mental note to ask more about Cajuns later. He seemed to recollect meeting a Cajun trapper once, but it had been when he was quite young and he couldn't remember much about the man or Cajuns in general.

The servant opened the carriage door and gave a courtly bow. *"Soyez le bienvenul,"* he said cordially.

Milhouse started to climb out first but Adam Tyler slapped the trapper's arm and nodded at Louisa. She eased past them. Much to her delight, the servant took her arm to help her down, bowing again as he did so.

"Bonjour Mademoiselle."

Lou didn't know what he was saying. To be polite she responded, "Howdy to you, too. Thank you very much for the help."

Tyler slid out next. *"Parlez-vous Anglais?"* he asked.

"Yes, sir, I do," the servant answered in thickly accented English. "I speak seven languages. French, English, Spanish, and some of the dialects of the African workers my master employs."

Zach couldn't get over it. The man knew seven languages and he was a *servant?* He made another mental note to ask Tyler about how people became servants. And why, for that matter, anyone would want to be one.

"My name is Jules. If you would be so kind as to follow me, I will escort you inside." As he led them up the marble stairs he inquired of the tall gambler, "Might I ask who you are and the nature of your visit? I will impart the information to Mr. Goujon."

"Tell him Adam Tyler has come calling."

"That's all, sir?"

"It's more than enough."

Jules opened the door to admit them. Louisa had been in a mansion before, but she was far from accustomed to such luxurious surroundings. Spectacular paintings lined the hallway. The hardwood floor shone with polish. Here and there were small mahogany tables, one bearing a gold lamp, while on another rested an exquisite sculpture of a dolphin and a woman leaping side by side through a curling wave. The women, to Lou's dismay, was portrayed naked.

Her mother, Lou reflected, would have been horror-struck. In their household they were never permitted to bare their bodies to one another. It was considered shameful. One time, when she was twelve, she had been taking a bath in big metal tub out back of their house and the wind loosened one of the sheets her ma hung up to grant her a measure of privacy. A neighbor boy, not much more than six years of age, happened to be playing in the next yard and saw her. Only part of her, mind. The upper half of her body. She had squealed and ducked lower in the tub, doing what she could to cover herself. It wasn't enough to suit her mother. She'd been punished severely, an injustice Lou never forgave.

"This way, please," Jules said, turning right down another long hall.

It was decorated with stuffed animal heads. Zach admired the rack of a white-tailed buck and the trophy of a huge black bear. He'd seen grizzlies twice its size, but he'd never seen anything stuffed and mounted before.

The parlor into which they were ushered was large enough to accommodate fifty people. A sparkling chandelier graced the vaulted ceiling, and green drapes framed a row of high windows. Costly furniture added to the opulence. Zach ran a finger over a long table and examined the tip. The table didn't have so much as a speck of dust on it.

George Milhouse made a *tsk-tsk* sound. "I could never

live in a place like this. The rooms are too darned big. If I want to hear an echo, I'd live in a cave."

Zach moved to a bookcase that had a shiny glass front and examined some of the titles. *Moby Dick. The Last of the Mohican. Ivanhoe,* naturally. *The Holy Bible.* All books Zach knew of. Several he didn't, such as *The Decline and Fall of the Roman Empire* and *The Complete Works of Plato.*

"Do you read, young man?"

Zach turned. Two men had entered. Both had handsome, leonine features and wore immaculate suits. One was decades older than the other, his hair flecked with grey, but otherwise they were spitting images of one another. Father and son, Zach guessed. The older one had addressed him. "Yes, I do. My pa taught me when I was knee-high to a buffalo calf. He always said reading broadened the mind. Many a winter's night he or my ma would crack a book and read us kids to sleep."

"You have wise parents, then. Reading is the cornerstone to wisdom, and as the Bible says, we must acquire wisdom before all else." The man bowed, then smiled. "Forgive me. I should have introduced myself first. I am Jacques Goujon. This handsome gallant behind me is my son, Auguste."

Jules stepped to one side and tucked his chin to his chest. "I was just coming to inform you of their arrival, sir."

"We saw them from an upstairs window," Jacques Goujon disclosed. "Please be so kind as to have the maids bring refreshments."

"Right away, sir."

Adam Tyler strode over with his right hand out. "It's nice to make your acquaintance at long last, Monsieur Goujon. I've heard many things about you. A lot of it from your son here."

"Monsieur Tyler," Jacques said, shaking warmly. *"Oui,* Auguste has also told me much about you. A man of honor, he calls you. There is no higher compliment."

Tyler shook the son's hand. "Good to see you again, Auguste."

"Same here, Adam, *mon ami*." Auguste bent at the waist.

Zach had never seen so much bowing and scraping in all his born days. Some white customs, he mused, were positively comical. Why, he'd heard tell that over in England and Europe men kissed the hands of ladies when they met. He could just see a Shoshone warrior kissing the hand of another warrior's wife! Blood would flow, for sure.

"I apologize for calling on you without an invitation," Adam said, "but we have an important matter to discuss."

"We do?" Jacques said. "Well, then, let us sit and get to it, as you Americans like to say." He motioned at nearby chairs and a sofa. "As for calling unannounced, think nothing of it. You are always welcome here and anyone you might bring with you." He turned. "Introductions are in order, are they not?"

The gambler did the honors. Louisa was tickled when both father and son dipped at the knees and kissed the back of her hand. She saw her beloved turn scarlet with jealousy and smiled to soothe his fiery temper.

Zach hadn't expected them to kiss Lou. He remembered a trapper mentioning once that the French were the kissingest bunch of folks who ever lived, and now he'd seen the proof with his own eyes. He half worried they might kiss him, but all they did was shake and welcome him to their home.

George Milhouse hobbled over, his usual smirk in place. "How-do, Mr. Goujon," he said grandiosely, energetically levering the Frenchman's arm as if it were the pump to a deep well. "Nice mansion you've got here." He deliberately stressed the word *mansion* while bestowing a smug glance on Lou.

"It has been in my family for generations," Jacques said.

"Do tell? That explains it."

"Explains what, monsieur?"

"How you folks find your way around without a map."

Both the Goujons laughed, the elder bidding the trapper to sit on the sofa. Milhouse, being his usual contrary self, chose a chair instead. Which suited Zach just fine. Taking Lou's elbow, he claimed the sofa for them. He didn't want either of the amorous Frenchmen within kissing range.

Just as everyone sat, someone else entered. Zach saw Adam Tyler's head snap around as if yanked by invisible hands. Swiveling, Zach beheld a vision of loveliness floating across the floor as if borne on a shimmering cloud. Her hair was blazing yellow, her complexion as smooth as the marble steps, her bearing regal. She was, quite simply, stunning. The rest of the men instantly stood back up so he did likewise.

Jacques Goujon embraced the newcomer. "Gentlemen. And Miss Clark. I would like you to meet the apple of my eye, my daughter, Celeste." One by one he introduced each of them.

Milhouse merely nodded at her, but Adam Tyler walked over, grasped her fingers as delicately as if they were fragile rose petals, and lowered his mouth to her alabaster knuckles.

"It's my extreme pleasure to meet you, Mademoiselle Goujon. I'd heard rumors of your sensational beauty, but until this moment I assumed the reports were exaggerated. Now I see that, if anything, they were understated."

Lou saw Celeste Goujon avert her eyes, then look directly into Tyler's. Lou sensed that the gambler's gushing compliment was more than formality, that Tyler was keenly attracted to the woman. She could be wrong, but Lou also sensed that Celeste reciprocated. None of the men seemed to notice, though, so Lou told herself it must be her imagination. Then again, where emotions were concerned, the males of the species were notoriously thickheaded.

Jacques introduced Lou. She judged Celeste to be in her late twenties, possibly early thirties, and took it for granted Celeste must have a husband. Most women Celeste's age did. But Jacques's next comment set her straight.

"My daughter has recently returned from France where she has been in mourning for almost a year. Her husband, Philippe de Bethune, the Duke of Sully, died in a most tragic accident."

Everyone was staring at Celeste except Lou. She was watching Adam Tyler. He offered condolences but his eyes gave lie to the words he uttered. Something about Celeste had stirred him mightily. It perplexed Lou. The gambler hadn't disclosed much about his personal life to her. But from what she gathered from Zach, Tyler had been in love once, a love that ended tragically, and as a result the gambler had shied away from women ever since.

At Jacques Goujon's bidding, they all sat back down. Celeste picked an empty chair near Tyler's.

"Now then," their host said. "Suppose we discuss the matter that brought the four of you here."

But they were interrupted again, this time by a pair of maids in pretty pink uniforms. One bore a tray laden with a teapot, a coffeepot, and cups. The other's tray was layered with various cheeses, meats, and crackers. Lou grinned when Adam Tyler asked Celeste what she would like and then poured a cup of tea for her.

"So," Jacques declared after everyone had chosen, "unless the ceiling caves in on us, I think we can get on with our business." He faced the gambler. "Perhaps you would be so kind as to tell me the nature of this urgency you alluded to."

"Racine."

Jacques, about to lift his cup, paused. "What about him? He has been indentured to me for years. A more dependable, decent man you will not find anywhere."

Zach fully intended to stay quiet and let Adam do most of the talking, as Adam wanted, but to hear Racine praised so highly rankled him. His leg was still sore where the manservant had kicked it. "Decent my eye. Do decent men traipse around peeking into windows in the middle of the night?"

Adam shot Zach a barbed gaze fraught with disapproval. "Forgive my young friend. He's spent most of his life in the Rocky Mountains and his manners aren't what they should be."

Jacques dismissed Zach's social blunder with a gesture. "What is this about Racine peeking into windows?"

"Into one of mine," Adam said.

"Into one of . . . ?" Jacques said, then he did the one thing Zach would never have foreseen. The elder Goujon laughed heartily, and to Zach's amazement, his son chimed in.

Adam was clearly irritated, but Lou saw him glance quickly at Celeste, compose himself, and say, "Why do you find this so humorous?"

Jacques nodded, then clapped his hands twice, loudly. Almost immediately Jules filled the doorway, awaiting instructions. "Find Racine. I believe he is out at the stable tending the new foal. Have him report here right away."

"Yes, sir." Jules wheeled and departed.

Louisa was having great fun observing the gambler and Celeste on the sly. The daughter had been studying him with great interest, and now she swung toward her father in a fit of pique.

"I think it frightfully rude, *mon pere,* to laugh at our guests without telling them why. Surely you can share the reason before Racine arrives?"

"I would never intentionally insult anyone, my dear," Jacques responded. "You should know me better than that." He smiled at Adam. "I laughed because the idea of Racine going around at night peeking into windows is quite funny. He is a remarkable man. His sense of honor, like your own, is impeccable. For him to engage in such a ludicrous pursuit only shows how devoted he is to one he is helping. I simply had no idea—" Jacques stopped and looked at his son, and they both laughed again.

Auguste found it even more entertaining than his father and struggled to keep a straight face. "You see, my friends,

Racine frowns on childish pastimes. He is always so serious about things. We hardly ever see him laugh. It is unthinkable for him to indulge acts he considers beneath his dignity, so to learn he has been spending his free time peeking into windows is quite comical."

"Don't get us wrong," Jacques hastily said. "Racine has a few quirks. But he is one of the finest men I have ever known. He should have been born into polite society, a gentleman by right of birth, but fate was cruel to him. He was born into abject poverty, the seventh son of a shiftless sharecropper who had twelve children in all."

Zach didn't see what any of that had to do with the man peeping into windows, but he'd already annoyed Adam once by speaking out of turn so he held his peace.

"Most men in his situation would never amount to much," Jacques said. "Racine was an exception. He rose above his station through much hard work and diligence. As a boy he attended school by doing work around the schoolhouse in return for books and whatever else was needed. He learned to take care of horses and other valuable skills. Then, at only fourteen years of age, he came to me with a most unique proposition."

George Milhouse, who had been uncommonly quiet, broke his silence. "Let me guess. He indentured himself to you?"

"*Oui*. He sold himself to me for a period of twenty years. For quite a substantial sum, I might add. Much more than I have ever paid for any other servant." Jacques paused. "You should have seen him. This boy in rags, marching boldly up to our door and requesting to see me. Then sitting across from me at my desk and calmly telling me that if I would agree to pay the sum he needed to help out his family, I would have the benefit of his services for the next two decades. His audacity was astounding. Ordinarily, I wouldn't have agreed. He was much too young. But even then I saw he was different. I saw something special deep in him, a quality that sets him apart from most men. So I agreed."

Zach's tongue moved of its own accord. "You made him your slave?"

It was Auguste who responded. "Slaves and indentured servants are not the same, Slaves are bought outright, like a horse or a cow, and are slaves for life. Indentured servants work under contract for a specified period of time. When that time is up, they are on their own again, free to do as they please."

"It stills sounds like a kind of slavery to me," Zach said.

Jacques grinned. "You have owned many slaves, have you?"

Zach didn't like the Frenchman's attitude. "I'd never own another person. But I met a slave once. Or, a former slave. He ran off because the man who owned him treated him and a bunch of others like animals. They had to live in filthy, run-down shacks. They were fed the same slop as the hogs. And their owner liked to whip them, over any little excuse at all."

"I am most sorry to hear that." Jacques sounded sincere. "Yes, there are plantation owners who treat their slaves despicably. But they are in the minority. Slaves cost money. To work them into the ground and abuse them is the same as throwing that money into the wind."

"Any kind of slavery is wrong," Zach commented.

"You would sit in judgement on an institution that has existed for hundreds if not thousands of years? For your information, young man, I treat my slaves decently. They are housed in log cabins. They are free to grow gardens in small plots I give them. I make sure they have adequate clothing. When they are sick, my own physician attends them. In short, I see that all their needs are met."

"So you can get your money's worth out of them."

"There is much more to it than that. But, yes, it makes

good business sense to keep them well fed, well clothed, and healthy."

Adam Tyler motioned at Zach, his meaning obvious. He wanted Zach to let the matter drop but Zach couldn't. "Doesn't it ever bother you, Mr. Goujon? Knowing you own other people?"

"It is how things are done, Monsieur King. How my father did them, and his father before him. How plantations are run throughout the entire southern half of the United States." Jacques pursed his lips. "To be honest, yes, there are days when I think that being lord and master to three hundred families is wrong. That I am not God. That I have no right." He gazed out the nearest high window at slaves toiling under the morning sun in a distant field. "But what else am I to do? Grant them their freedom? That would be a calamity."

"Why?" Zach asked.

"They are ill equipped to live in the outside world. Most would be forced to take work that pays a pittance. The conditions they would live under would be much worse than those they live under here." Goujon folded his hands on his knee. "And where would I find workers to replace them? No white man would stoop to labor in the fields. And indentured workers prefer domestic work. No, I am afraid the status quo is best for everyone involved."

Zach still didn't agree. To him, nothing in life was more important then being free. The Shoshones and other tribes, the mountain men—they all believed that no one had the right to tell another what to do. And when all the fancy talk about slavery was stripped away, that was what it boiled down to.

There was a commotion at the door. Jules entered, out of breath. Behind him strode another man in a dark brown suit, a man with a hooked nose and hawkish features, features Zach knew all to well.

"Racine!" Jacques declared. "Thank you for joining us."

David Thompson

But the Cajun seemed not to hear. Suddenly rushing forward, he clasped Louisa by the shoulders and bodily lifted her from the sofa. *"Mon Dieu!* It was you last night! Your back was to me and I couldn't be sure. I have found you at last!"

Chapter Four

Zachary King was on his feet before he quite realized what he was doing. His hand dropped to the hilt of his bowie. All the blood had rushed to his head and his temples were pounding.

No conscious thought directed him. Zach only knew the hawk-faced man had his hands on Lou, and he didn't like it, he didn't like it one bit. With a flick of his wrist, the big knife swished from its beaded sheath.

Louisa May Clark was dumfounded by the newcomer's strange behavior. She had never set eyes on him before yet he acted as if he had met her somewhere. His strong grip and the intent glint in his eyes alarmed her, but it was nothing compared to the stark fear that coursed through her when, over Racine's shoulder, she beheld the love of her life lunge.

St. Louis wasn't the Rockies. In the mountains conflicts

were common, and men often settled them with a knife or a gun. The loser was buried, the winner went on with his life, and that was that. In St. Louis conflicts were also common, but since polite society frowned on bloodshed, the winners frequently wound up in prison or were sent to the gallows.

Louisa lived in daily dread that Zach's fiery temper might result in his being thrown behind bars or worse. Now, seeing the look on his face, she was afraid he would murder Racine on the spot. "Zach!" she cried out. "No!"

Zach barely heard her. He was focused on the Cajun to the exclusion of all else. He saw Racine spin, incredibly fast, saw the man start to dodge, but Zach was faster. Seizing the Cajun's arm, he streaked the long blade at Racine's throat.

Lou screamed.

Zach never meant to kill the man, though. Racine was unarmed and posed no serious threat. Zach just wanted him to take his hands off Lou. So rather than separate the Cajun's head from his body, Zach checked his swing a fraction of an instant before the bowie sheared into Racine's neck.

The Cajun froze.

"That's my fiancée you're manhandling," Zach said through clenched teeth. "I'd be obliged if you'd keep your paws to yourself."

Louisa, like everyone else, was frozen in place. She couldn't make up her mind whether to be mad at Zach for being so ill-mannered or proud at how quickly he had leaped to her defense, even though she hadn't really needed protecting.

No one said a word. Racine himself broke the tense stillness by gazing squarely at Zach and saying, without a trace of fright or resentment, "I am sorry. I permitted my happiness to carry me away. Please forgive me. I meant no harm."

Zach's anger evaporated like morning mist under a hot

sun. Slowly lowering the bowie, he said, "I reckon I got a little carried away, too." Twirling the knife, he sheathed the big blade with a flourish.

George Milhouse chortled. "That's my boy! He reminds me of me when I was green behind the ears."

Auguste was also impressed. "*Magnifique!* I have never seen such speed, such control. I thought for sure Monsieur King would take Racine's head off."

Lou, smoothing her dress, noted that Adam Tyler had stepped in front of Celeste as if to shield her should a fight erupt. "I about had a conniption," she joked, seeking to divert attention from Zach. "I wish someone would tell me what this is all about."

The elder Goujon was more upset by his manservant's behavior than anything else. "Racine, that was uncalled for. Monsieur King would be within his rights to challenge you to meet him on Bloody Island. And I dare say, if the weapon chosen is knives, he might well prove your better."

Racine bowed his head to Zach. "Is that your wish, monsieur? You have only to pick the time, and I will be there at the appointed hour, with my seconds, of course."

Zach, at a complete loss, glanced at Adam.

"He wants to know if you would like to challenge him to a duel," the gambler clarified. "Bloody Island is the local field of honor, you might say. Gentlemen with grievances go there to resolve disputes. It's out in the middle of the Mississippi and can only be reached by boat."

"A duel?" The notion had never entered Zach's head. He'd heard about the white custom from his father, who liked to tell the story of the time Andrew Jackson took part in one. But it would never occur to Zach to settle a problem that way.

Tyler wasn't done. "It's a grave breech of etiquette for one man to lay a hand on another's wife or sweetheart. Not that anyone has ever kept count, but more duels have been fought over women than anything else."

"Challenge him, boy!" George Milhouse said. "I've always wanted to see a duel but never had the chance."

Lou couldn't tell if the old trapper was kidding or not, but she answered before Zach could to nip the idea in the bud. "There won't be any duels fought over me. If any man goes too far, I'll shoot him my own self."

Celeste was astounded. "You would do that, mademoiselle?"

"Sure. Why not? It's not like I haven't shot men before."

"White men?"

"What difference does their color make? Whether they're white or red or purple, if they're fixing to make wolf meat of me they deserve a slug between the eyes." The last man Lou had shot had been trying to kill her and Zach's little sister, Evelyn. The fact he'd been white had nothing to do with it.

Which was ironic. There had been a time, Lou reflected, when she wouldn't think of harming a fly, let alone another human being. As a small girl she'd often cried if anyone so much as raised their voice to her. She couldn't stand conflict, couldn't abide violence. When her ma and pa argued, as they sometimes did, she'd go hide out in her room until the storm passed.

When her father, Zebulon, had proposed venturing into the remote Rockies to trap beaver, Lou had been against the plan. Not because the family had to travel hundreds of miles through country overrun with fierce beasts and savage men, but because she couldn't bear the thought of harmless beaver being trapped and skinned.

Her pa had been adamant. Raising plews, as the mountaineers called it, would earn them more money in a single year than Zebulon could make in a decade. It proved a fateful decision. Lou's ma died on the trek west, and her pa was later slain by a war party. Lou had been left all alone in the world—until Zach came along.

Celeste Goujon couldn't get over it. "I have never heard of a woman who has killed. Yet you are so young, so . . . ordinary."

"Oh, thanks," Lou said sarcastically.

"Non, non. I didn't not mean it the way it sounded. You are ordinary in that you are a pretty young girl. Never in a million years would I suspect you had ever shot anyone."

Lou shrugged. "Maybe if you saw me in my buckskins you'd be more inclined to believe it." Only then did it sink in how much she had truly changed. To talk about killing people as offhandedly as she might tell about swatting a fly or crushing a mosquito was outrageous. And yet, if she hadn't mustered the courage, if she hadn't defended herself, she wouldn't be standing there having the discussion.

"Ladies, ladies," Jacques interjected. "All of this is quite fascinating, but Monsieur Tyler and Monsieur King are awaiting Racine's explanation."

Zach reclaimed his seat. The business about duels had stuck in his mind. He seemed to recollect Shakespeare McNair saying his own father had fought one once, a long time ago. But it wasn't something his pa saw fit to mention.

"Where to begin?" Racine said. "I suppose it all started a couple of weeks ago when I was in the city one evening, on one of my two days off each month. I was passing by the Grand Imperial Hotel when I heard women shout for help."

Lou straightened. "The Grand Imperial?"

"Oui, mademoiselle. Two young ladies were beside a gentleman who had been knocked to the ground. I ran over to be of help. One of them pointed at a scoundrel who had just stolen their traveling bags and was running off."

"A footpad," Jacques said in disgust.

"I chased him," Racine detailed. "We scuffled, and I was able to retrieve the bags. The young ladies and the gentleman, their father, were most grateful. They invited me to dine with them, and later took me to their suite at the Imperial for drinks. During the course of our conversation they mentioned how they had come to St. Louis from Ohio to meet with a relative they had not seen for a long time—"

Zach glanced at his sweetheart.

"—but that they had not heard from her and they were afraid she might never show. They planned to stay at the Imperial the entire month, waiting." Racine paused. "The next morning I told my master about the encounter. Monsieur Goujon graciously offered to have them stay here instead of at the hotel. When I relayed the news, they were hesitant at first but they finally accepted. They have been here ever since, waiting and hoping."

It was obvious who the Cajun was referring to. Questions gushed from Lou in a torrent. "My Aunt Martha is here? And Uncle Thomas and everyone else? Where are they now? Why didn't they leave word at the Imperial? And what does all this have to do with you peeking into Adam's window?"

Racine smiled. "*Oui*, mademoiselle, they are all here. Your Aunt Martha, her husband, and Harry. Also your Uncle Thomas, Ethel, and Gladys."

Happiness brought Lou to her feet. "Then what are you waiting for? Take me to them."

"Would that I could," Racine said, "but they are off exploring the city. They like to visit the shops and stores. And lovely Gladys is fond of the sun."

Lou thought that was a strange comment to make but she was too excited to give it much thought. "They're staying here," she repeated in disbelief.

Jacques Goujon chuckled. "You are pleased, *non?* I recognized your name when we were introduced and would have told you myself, but I knew your relatives or Racine would rather have the honor. Please forgive me."

"There's nothing to forgive," Lou said.

Zach didn't share his fiancée's joy. He was extremely nervous about meeting her kin. Time and again Lou had assured him they would like him but what if they didn't?

"As for the window," Racine began to explain, "your aunt did leave word for you at the hotel. And every day, without fail, one of them has gone to the Imperial to check if you have been by."

"But Zach and I did go there," Lou said. "The desk clerk told me they had checked out, and he said nothing about any note."

"A most unfortunate circumstance," Racine said. "Gladys and I apparently stopped by less than fifteen minutes after you left. We learned you had just been there. But the clerk on duty that day was new to his job. He didn't look in the proper slot. Your aunt's message was there the whole time."

George Milhouse rapped his cane on the floor. "All this is well and good, mister. But if you don't get to why you were peekin' in that window sometime this century, I'm liable to bust."

"Bear with me, please. I was in the city, making inquiries, trying to find out where Mademoiselle Clark was staying. All everyone was talking about was Lon Festerman's death. Many rumors were being spread. Among them was one that a prominent gambler maybe had a hand in it." Racine looked at Tyler. "Another rumor had it that a beautiful young woman was involved, a young woman recently arrived from the far off Rockies."

"I get it!" Lou exclaimed. "You put two and two together and figured I was staying with Adam."

"Well, I hoped Adam might have information on your whereabouts," Racine replied. "My only problem was that Adam had never told me where he lived. And since he is so secretive by nature, hardly anyone else knew, either. Finally a mutual friend of ours, Henry LeBeau, gave me three possible addresses. Adam had told him once, long ago, but Henri couldn't remember which of the three it might be."

"So you went to each one, skulking around like a damn fool?" George Milhouse said. "Why in tarnation didn't you just come to the front door and knock?"

"At that time of night? To call unannounced would be unthinkable." Racine clasped his hands behind his back. "Yours was the second house I visited. When I saw Mademoiselle Clark, I thought it might be her. But I didn't want to say anything to Gladys and the others until I confirmed it, which I intended to do this evening."

"Wait a minute," Zach said. "Why didn't you say something when Adam and I caught up with you?"

The Cajun sighed. "You attacked me without identifying yourselves. All I knew was that two men were chasing me. It was dark and I did not get a good look at either of you. I thought I could reach the carriages and go my way, but you, Monsieur King, run like the wind. You caught up and we fought. When Adam reached us and aimed his derringer at me, I reacted without thinking."

"But Adam spoke to you," Zach said.

"Oui. But in the heat of the moment I did not recognize his voice. And with his hat pulled so low over his face—" Racine shrugged. "I assumed you were robbers."

"All three of you were fortunate," Jacques said. "It could have ended in tragedy."

Racine bowed slightly at Zach and Louisa. "Now you know everything. Your relatives should be back by three this afternoon. I'm sure my master won't mind if you wait."

"Not at all," Jacques said. "We would be honored to have your company." He stood. "In fact, if the two of you would like, you are welcome to stay here with us for the duration of your visit to St. Louis."

"Oh, we couldn't," Lou automatically said.

"Why not, pray tell, mademoiselle? From what I understand, you haven't seen your aunt or the rest for almost two years. Every minute spent with them is precious, is it not?"

"Yes, but—"

"But nothing. I insist." Jacques smiled. "We have plenty of spare rooms, and my servants will see to your every need. So you can't claim it would be an inconvenience."

Zach hoped Lou declined. He liked staying at Adam's. And, too, the thought of being with her relatives twenty-four hours a day compounded his nervousness.

Celeste also rose. "Oh, please agree, Mademoiselle

Clark! It would be wonderful! What great fun we could have with Ethel and Gladys."

"Call me Lou," Louisa requested. She came to a spur-of-the-moment decision. "Sure. Why not? Like you say, Mr. Goujon, I haven't seen any of them in a coon's age. I suppose I should make the most of it." She glanced down at Zach. "You don't mind, do you, darling?"

"Not at all," Zach lied. But what else could he do? He loved her and would do anything for her. Swallow nails. Jump off a cliff. Live under the same roof with her kinfolk. "I can't wait to meet them."

George Milhouse tittered. "All's well that ends well, then. Thank God. I haven't heard this much jabberin' since my third wife went on a spiel about me keepin' our lodge tidy." His forehead furrowed. "Or was it my fourth wife? Sometimes I tend to forget which was which. One of them had a big butt, I remember that much."

Adam Tyler made a sound like a dog being strangled. "I'm sure our hosts don't care to hear about the physical attributes of your many women."

Auguste Goujon was gaping at the old trapper. "Did I hear correctly, monsieur? You have had *four* wives?"

"I thought about havin' a fifth but I was tired of outlivin' every gal who caught my fancy. Plus, the naggin' sort of got to me after fifty years."

"Four women at once?" Auguste said.

"Lordy, no. What do you think I am, a glutton for punishment?" Milhouse snickered. "I knew a fella who had two wives at once, though. Crows, they were. Cutest girls you ever did see. On cold nights he'd lie between them and—"

"Enough," Adam Tyler said a trifle sternly. "Need I remind you there are ladies present?"

"So? All I was going to say is that he liked to tickle 'em with a feather. They laughed so damn loud, they'd wake up half the village."

"Remarkable," Jacques commented.

"Barbaric," Racine said.

Auguste walked over to the mountain man. "Tell me, Monsieur Milhouse. To your knowledge, do Crow women ever visit St. Louis? I would very much like to meet a few."

Everyone paired off and began talking at once. Lou and Racine. Adam and Celeste. Milhouse and Auguste. Zach was left to himself, alone on the sofa, feeling neglected and dreading that Louisa had made a mistake in agreeing to Jacques's invitation. He saw the elder Goujon leave the room. Sinking back against the cushions, fighting off a wave of depression, he scolded himself for being childish. The Livingstons and the Clarks would accept him into the family with open arms. Isn't that what Lou kept saying?

A sudden intense longing for the mountains seized him. Zach gazed out the west window. Silhouetted on the horizon were St. Louis's tallest buildings. How small and insignificant they were, he reflected, compared with the towering, regal Rockies. He wished he was back among them, with Lou at his side.

Fond recollections stirred Zach's soul. A month or so before they left, they'd gone to a remote meadow to spend time alone. Lou brought food in a parfleche, and after tying their horses, they spread out a blanket beside a gurgling stream. They'd kissed a while, then Zach stretched out on his back and she had nestled in his arms, her cheek on his chest.

Zach remembered the sweet smell of her hair, the scent of the green grass, the sound of the swiftly flowing water. He remembered the warmth of the sun on his face, and the warmth of her body against his. It had been utter bliss.

For long, lazy minutes Zach had played with Louisa's hair, running his fingers through it and curling it around her small ear. Eventually she'd dozed and Zach had held her close, marveling that she cared for him. He could never understand why, which made the gift of her love that much more extraordinary. What was it about him that attracted her? he'd wondered. Why, of all the men she'd ever met, had she bestowed her heart on him and him alone? What, exactly, was *love?*

Later Zach asked his father about it. His pa had smiled in that kindly way his pa had, then said, "Love is one of the great mysteries of life, son. I don't pretend to know why two people fall in love. They just do."

"So I'll never know why Lou cares for me?"

"Be glad she does and let it go at that. Some things don't bear looking into too deeply. Love is one of them. The harder you try to understand it, the less you will."

"That doesn't make any kind of sense, Pa."

"People have been saying the same since the beginning of the human race, I suspect." Nate had stared overhead at the myriad brilliant stars. "Love is like creation, son. There's a lot more to it than we can see. It does us no good to try and understand it, because it's beyond understanding."

Like most fathers and sons, Zach and his pa had experienced their share of spats. Maybe more than their share. His father was disappointed in his attitude toward most whites, but then his father had never endured the rank prejudice Zach did. They also argued constantly over Zach's long-cherished goal to count more coup than any Shoshone warrior ever had or ever would. Nate never said as much, but Zach believed his pa thought he was a bit too bloodthirsty, a bit too violent.

Be that as it may, Zach had to give his father proper due. Nate King had a justly deserved reputation for being as honest as the year was long, for being fair in all his dealings with others no matter what color their skin might be, and for always being loyal to his family and friends.

Zach would add one more important quality to that list. His pa was wiser than most ten men combined. Next to Shakespeare McNair, Zach's father was the wisest man Zach knew. That was why, when Zach was troubled, when there was an important question he couldn't answer, or if he simply needed an open ear, he always turned to his father.

Zach had never felt very comfortable baring his feelings to his mother. He couldn't quite say why. His ma was as loving as woman as ever lived, as loving as his father, even more so in some respects. Yet, try as he might, when it came to deeply personal issues, Zach couldn't open up to her.

So it surprised Zach all that more that he could do so with Louisa. Revealing his innermost feelings to her came as naturally as breathing. From the day they'd met, he'd never held anything back.

With one exception.

Zach had never shared his special dread over meeting Lou's aunt and uncle. He was scared to death, yet he wouldn't say a word for fear of angering or insulting Lou. It scared him more than anything. More than the prospect of encountering a grizzly. More than battling a Blackfoot war party. More than being captured by Bloods.

Zach's fear was illogical. It was irrational. It was silly. Yet, despite knowing all that, he couldn't shake it, couldn't suppress it, couldn't conquer it. It gnawed at him like a festering wound. It stripped him of his reason, of his common sense.

What made it even harder to endure was that such unreasoning fear flew in the face of everything Zach believed in. He was a Shoshone warrior, and Shoshone warriors did not give in to their fears. True warriors mastered them. Real warriors faced hardship without flinching, faced conflict with courage.

Now, staring at the silhouette of St. Louis in the distance, Zach longed to get away from there before the inevitable meeting took place. He yearned to be back in that meadow, just Lou and him, as they had been on that glorious spring day. No conflicts. No storm clouds looming. No aunts and uncles he had never met. Just Louisa, dozing on his chest, the sun warm on their bodies, life as sweet as it ever got.

"—listening to me?"

Zach became aware his fiancée had been speaking to him. "Sorry," he said. "I was thinking. What did you say?"

"Thinking about what?" Lou asked. The expression on his face showed he was troubled.

"Oh, about an elk hunt my pa and I went on some years back," Zach lied for the second time in twice as many minutes.

Lou leaped to the conclusion he was bored. Why else would he be daydreaming about a hunt that took place years ago? "I mentioned your interest in that fancy foot fighting to Racine. He says he'll be glad to sponsor you at the club he goes to."

Zach pushed erect. "You'd do that for me?" he asked the Cajun. "After I held a knife to your throat? And attacked you last night?"

"All due to misunderstandings," the Cajun said. "It would be my pleasure to sponsor you, Monsieur King. My instructor, Monsieur Chagall, is always on the lookout for students with promise. And with your reflexes, you would be a natural at savate."

Zach was flattered but didn't let on. "When can we visit your club?"

"I go twice a week without fail. Sometimes three." Racine pivoted and adopted that strange stance. "A practitioner of *la boxe Francaise* must keep his limbs flexible and conditioned at all times." Racine unfurled. "But enough about savate. The grand moment has arrived. The two of you must be very happy."

"What grand moment?" Zach asked.

Racine pointed out a window. "Why, your fiancée's reunion with her relatives. They are back sooner than I expected."

Coming up the winding gravel drive was a glittering carriage.

Chapter Five

Zachary King had been charged by fifteen-hundred pound bull buffalo, their wicked curved horns lowered to rip and rend, their heavy hooves hammering like thunder. He had been attacked by vicious mountain lions, their claws ready to slice him to ribbons. He had been set upon by roaring, slavering grizzlies, the demonic lords of the dark woods. Yet nothing in his experience compared to the awful, heart-freezing moment when the ornate carriage and its four-horse team of magnificent white geldings came to a halt in front of the Goujon mansion.

Zach broke out in a cold sweat even though, internally, he felt as hot as an inferno. It was as if he had a fever and the chills simultaneously. His mouth became as dry as a desert. When he tried to swallow, to muster saliva to wet his lips, he couldn't. His throat had become so constricted, it felt as if a solid lump were wedged tight.

As if all that weren't enough, Zach's palms became so damp he wiped them on his pants so when he shook hands his nervousness wouldn't be apparent. He felt awkward, inadequate, as out of place as a fish out of water or a moose in a china shop. His knees started to shake, and it was all he could do to keep from collapsing.

It was silly. It was stupid. It was ridiculous. Worst of all, it was totally unacceptable behavior for a Shoshone warrior. But Zach couldn't stop his traitorous body from reacting as it did although he railed at it mentally, seeking to regain some measure of self-control. He saw Louisa dash down the steps and braced himself.

Lou was giddy with joy. She hadn't realized just how much she missed her relations. Tears of elation moistened her eyes, and she pressed her hands to her bosom in excited expectation.

The carriage wasn't a rental. Racine had remarked, as they filed from the parlor, that it was owned by the Goujon family. A twelve-quarter coach, he'd called it. Like everything else the Goujon's possessed, it was lavish in the extreme. The four white horses were splendid animals, their manes and tails finely curried, their harness glittering with silver studs. The plum-colored carriage was one of the largest, if not *the* largest, Lou had ever beheld. Fully a third again as big as a normal conveyance, it was immaculate. Every square inch of wood had been polished to a gleaming shine. The same with every bit of metal. Perched in the driver's seat was a white-haired gentleman in a smart uniform the same color as the coach. In his high hat and knee-high black boots, he was quite picturesque himself.

"Pardon me, Mademoiselle Clark."

Jules hastened past to open the door.

Breathlessly, Lou quivered as a slender hand emerged. Jules, bowing, took it, and a small foot in a fashionable shoe lowered onto the passenger step attached to the underside of the carriage. A young woman about Lou's age appeared, her flowing dress almost the same shade as her curly russet hair. An oval face was lifted toward the mansion. Lively brown eyes swept those waiting above.

Lou thought those eyes fixed on Racine for a moment, then they shifted toward her and a piercing squeal rent the air.

"Louisa! Can it be? Is it really you?"

"Gladys!" Lou cried, bounding down, not caring one whit whether she was being ladylike or not. Her cousin awaited her with outflung arms, and they embraced warmly.

"I can't believe it! I can't believe it!" Gladys said over and over.

They drew apart to look at one another but Lou had hardly taken in the fact that her childhood chum had blossomed to become positively gorgeous when another woman practically leaped from the coach. Slightly older, she had darker hair and a darker dress but the same oval face and dancing eyes.

"Louisa! You little hussy!"

Lou was squeezed like a sponge and bodily lifted off the ground. "Ethel!" she whooped as she was spun around and then held at arm's length.

"Look at you!" Ethel declared. "Set anyone's britches on fire lately? Or doused the postman with water?"

Laughing, Lou clapped her on the shoulder. "Same old Ethel! You've got it backwards, as usual!"

Lou couldn't count the number of times her older cousin had gotten Gladys and her into hot water when they were little. Ethel was always the playful imp, the sprite who enjoyed playing practical jokes, the saucy rebel whose overly inquisitive nature had drawn the three of them into many glorious adventures, such as the time they snuck off to attend a visiting traveling carnival against their parents's wishes.

Gladys put a hand on each of them. "It's like old times! The three of us together again! Oh, I can't tell you how happy this makes me!"

Get Four Books Totally
F R E E* —
A Value between
$16 and $20

Tear here and mail your FREE* book card today!

- -

**PLEASE RUSH
MY FOUR FREE*
BOOKS TO ME
RIGHT AWAY!**

LeisureWestern Book Club
P.O. Box 6613
Edison, NJ 08818-6613

"Now, now, ladies. You'd think all of you were ten years old again."

Someone else had stepped down from the carriage. She, too, had an oval face, but hers bore the stamp of her well-nigh fifty years in the crinkles around her dark eyes and the deep lines around her mouth. Her expression was unduly stern given the circumstances, her dress a drab gray. Yet when she grinned, as she now did, she radiated genuine warmth. "My darling little niece," she said fondly.

"Aunt Martha!" Louisa threw herself into the older woman's arms, awash in childhood memories of being read bedtime tales while being rocked to sleep in her aunt's lap, of her aunt and her mother forever laughing and joking.

"It's wonderful to see you again, child," Aunt Martha said huskily, then pushed Lou back to study her. "Still small for your age, aren't you? And where did you get that awful dress? Doesn't that scatterbrained father of yours know that young ladies shouldn't wear potato sacks?"

Lou had forgotten how ungodly blunt her aunt could be. But in her happiness at seeing all of them again, she overlooked the crass comments and prepared to break the bad news about her father, Zebulon. Before she could, a straight-arrow man in a neatly ironed suit climbed down. Unlike the others, he didn't embrace her.

"Louisa. It's nice to see you again."

"Uncle Earnest."

Earnest Livingston was Martha's husband. By profession he was a lawyer, by disposition a notorious skinflint, as tight with money as he was with his emotions. Lou had never grown close to Earnest because he held everyone at a distance. What Aunt Martha saw in him, Lou never had understood.

Next to emerge was Harry Livingston, Lou's other cousin, son of Martha and Earnest. He was more sturdily built, big boned and long limbed, his ruddy complexion complementing his outgoing, friendly nature. "Louisa!" he roared, hugging her and swinging her in a circle. "Boy, it's great to see you again!"

Out of the corner of an eye Lou saw Earnest Livingston frown. It was no secret the man didn't hold the fruit of his loins in high esteem. Harry was his own flesh and blood, yet Earnest regarded him as a simpleton.

The tension between father and son had not reared its ugly head until Harry was in his late teens. That was when it became apparent to everyone that Harry would never follow in Earnest's footsteps. Harry was a decent, lovable sort, but his intellect wasn't what Earnest had hoped it would be. Once Earnest realized his son would never be admitted to the bar, Earnest erected a wall between them that, to Lou's knowledge, had never been breeched.

"Out of my way! Let me see her for myself! Move! Move!" Last to bounce down was Thomas Clark, father to Ethel and Gladys, brother to Lou's pa, Zebulon. A portly bundle of energy and affection, he shouldered Earnest and Harry aside and squeezed Louisa tight. "Lou, Lou, Lou! Look at you. As adorable as ever."

"Uncle Thomas!"

Up on the marble steps, his anxiety mounting by the moment, Zach wished the earth would split open and swallow him whole. In a few moments Lou would introduce him. He had a foolish urge to check his cravat, adjust his jacket, make sure his pants were free of lint. But his body locked up on him. He was unable to move, unable to even speak, in dire dread of the inevitable.

From the portico Jacques Goujon called down, "Come inside, everyone! It is too hot to stand out in the sun getting acquainted."

The Livingstons and the Clarks bustled upward. Earnest Livingston glanced at Zach, so Zach opened his mouth to introduce himself.

"Here, boy. Take care of this for me, will you?" The lawyer shoved his hat into Zach's outstretched hand. "That's a good fellow."

With a start, Zach realized Livingston mistook him for a servant. He went to set the man straight but the whole party swept on by, Lou caught in their midst like a piece of driftwood in a wave. She smiled at Zach and he smiled in return but he didn't feel like smiling. Within seconds they were all indoors, Adam Tyler and George Millhouse too, leaving him alone in the middle of the wide expanse of marble. Well, almost alone.

"Something wrong, sir?" Jules was on the next step down.

"No, no. I'm fine," Zach said absently.

"I'll take care of that hat, sir, if you don't mind," the servant said. He wiped some dust off the rim. "May I speak freely, sir?"

"Sure," Zach said. He couldn't get over being left there by himself, as if he were no consequence whatsoever.

"I noticed the mistake Monsieur Livingston made. Don't let it bother you. It's only normal for someone like him to think people like us are—" Jules paused. "How shall I put this, sir?"

"Worms under their feet," Zach said bitterly.

"Oh, no, sir. It's nothing like that. Monsieur Livingston just didn't think, is all. With your hair and your skin, anyone might have jumped to the same conclusion."

"I wouldn't have. Neither would you, I bet." Zach fought to contain his temper.

"Do me a favor from now on, Jules."

"Anything, sir."

"Don't ever call me that again. My handle is Zach. Or use Stalking Coyote, my Shoshone name. But no more 'sirs.' Is that clear?"

"Monsieur Goujon requires his servants to address guests formally," Jules said, "and I don't mind. Honest. Compared to a few other landowners I could mention, he's a kindhearted master. Being indentured to him was a stroke of luck."

Zach turned toward the Cajun. "Doesn't it ever get under

your skin? Having to wait on people hand and foot, I mean?"

"I am a servant, Monsieur King. Waiting on people is what I do. My work, if you will."

"But you're not free. You can't come and go as you please. You're always at Goujon's beck and call. I don't see how you stand it."

"I get two days off a month to do as I want," Jules said. "And what else would I do? Work at the docks? Sweep floors? Maybe learn a trade and be a blacksmith or a tinker?"

"You know fifty languages, for crying out loud. You must be awful smart. You could do whatever you want."

Jules smiled. "I only know seven. And I learned those in large part because Monsieur Goujon encouraged me to do so once he discovered I had an aptitude for it. He likes his servants to be the best they can possibly be."

"I just don't see how you stand it," Zach reiterated, heading indoors. Laughter and the hubbub of voices led him to the parlor. Louisa was surrounded by her kinfolk, all of them as merry as could be at their long-overdue reunion. Zach took several steps, then stopped. He felt as if he would be intruding, as if he were an outsider who had no rightful business being there.

Lou had been whisked inside so abruptly, she hadn't had an opportunity to tell her relatives the awful news yet. Ethel was sharing an amusing account of the time they had found a beehive and poked at it with sticks, trying to get honey, only to rile the bees and end up fleeing from a huge swarm.

"I was stung four times, I think. Gladys was stung twice. And little Louisa was stung something like eight times, mostly on her backside."

"Oh, how you screamed," Gladys said.

They all laughed, even Aunt Martha. When the hilarity subsided, Uncle Thomas cleared his throat and said, "Enough reminiscing, if you don't mind. Where the blazes is Zeb? Shouldn't my brother have joined us by now?"

"Yes, where is Zebulon?" Earnest said, looking around. "Is he hiding somewhere? Maybe he doesn't want to have to own up to his mistake, to his preposterous idea that he could make a lot of money at the beaver trade. It was as addlepated as all his other crazy schemes."

All eyes swung toward Lou. The moment had come, but she hesitated, reluctant to burst their happy bubble. She'd had more than a year to accept her father's fate; the others would be justly horrified. Taking a deep breath, she declared, "My pa is dead."

Stunned silence greeted the revelation.

"How's that again, dear?" Aunt Martha said.

"Hostiles killed him and took all our plews, the spring before last." Lou was unable to go into more detail. The memory was difficult enough to bear as it was.

The reality hit them and shock set in. Uncle Thomas bowed his head in sorrow. Ethel and Gladys gripped one another. Harry was crestfallen.

"I warned him," Aunt Martha said. "I warned him time and again of the perils he was exposing all of you to, but he wouldn't listen."

"Zeb never took advice," Earnest stated. "He always was a hardhead. Had to learn things for himself, was how he always put it. Well, look at what he reaped."

"First Marcy," Aunt Martha said, alluding to her sister, "and now Zebulon. Thank God you survived, Louisa."

"The Indians let me live because I was female," Lou responded.

Uncle Thomas took it hardest. Grief-stricken, he staggered to a chair. "I can't hardly believe it. Zeb, gone? My own brother! Why, it seems like only yesterday that he and I would sneak down to the quarry on a hot summer's day for a dip in the water pit. He always was a dreamer, though, always searching for the rainbow over the next horizon."

"There are no pots of gold at the end of rainbows," Earnest commented.

Lou would have liked to hit the lawyer over the head with a rock. The man had ice for a heart and less tact than a drunk. "We caught a lot of beaver, I'll have you know!" she snapped, close to crying. "Prime peltries, they were. Enough that when we sold them, we'd have had enough money to tide us through to the next trapping season and leave us a couple hundred dollars ahead."

Earnest held his hands up with the palms outward. "Easy, there. No need to bite my head off. I liked your father, remember?"

Did he really? Lou mused. Earnest always treated her pa as if Zeb were somehow inferior. "Don't ever speak ill of him. Not one of you, hear?"

Harry draped a brawny arm across her shoulders. "Easy there. Calm down, Lou. We're family. We all feel sorry for you."

Aunt Martha tenderly patted Lou's wrist. "That's right, little one. We'll help you pick up the pieces and get on with your life. I'll take you under my wing as if you were my own child and give you the benefit of my guidance from here on out."

"I'm not a child," Lou said defensively.

"True," Earnest said. "But we would be remiss in our responsibility to your dear mother's memory if we didn't insure your future happiness."

Ethel and Gladys also oozed sympathy. "How did you ever make it all the way back here on your own?" the former asked.

"What have you been doing with yourself since?" quizzed the latter. "How have you made ends meet? Weren't you afraid, being all alone in a bawdy city like St. Louis? Women aren't safe here on the streets after dark. Why, a footpad accosted our father and us right in front of our hotel."

Lou pried loose of Harry and her aunt and took a step back. "There's something else you should know." She would rather wait until a better time but circumstances dictated otherwise. "I don't live in St. Louis. I live up in the Rockies—"

"You what?" Aunt Martha's astonishment was a perfect reflection of that mirrored by everyone else.

"Are you insane, girl?" Earnest said. "The mountains are even less suitable for a young lady than St. Louis. Why, your own father was murdered by savages, yet you stay up there all alone?"

"I'm not alone," Lou said. "I've been staying with a family who took me in—"

"Indians?" Aunt Martha interrupted.

"No. Yes. Well, the wife is, but her husband is white. Nate King is his name, and he was a free trapper once. Now he mainly works as a guide. Winona, his wife, is Shoshone. They have a son slightly older than me and a daughter who is—"

Again Aunt Martha broke in. "He's a mountain man, is that what you're saying? From what we've heard, they live like savages themselves."

Lou glanced over her aunt's shoulder and spied Zach. Anxious to introduce him and to keep Martha from spouting more nonsense about mountaineers, she blurted much louder than was called for, "I'm engaged to Nate King's son, Zachary. He came to St. Louis with me, and I'd like to introduce him." Grinning to hide her unease, she beckoned to her sweetheart.

Zach stepped forward, his skin prickling as as if from a heat rash, his heart pounding like a hammer on an anvil. His palms grew damp once more and his mouth uncomfortably dry. The Livingstons and the Clarks scrutinized him closely. Uncle Thomas showed no emotion except continued sorrow over the death of his brother. Ethel and Gladys were openmouthed with amazement. Harry smiled. But Uncle Earnest was as impassive as a blank slate. That left Aunt Martha, whose dark eyes seemed to gleam like those of a wolf's in the glow of flickering firelight.

"I'm pleased to meet all of you," Zach said, his voice

sounding strained even to him. He was supremely thankful Adam Tyler had given him the store-bought clothes. At least he would make a fairly good impression.

For tense seconds none of them moved. Then Aunt Martha accepted his hand, saying, "Zachary, is it? A fine Christian name."

Earnest shook without comment, his mouth pinched together as if he had just sucked on a lemon.

Ethel and Gladys began giggling like schoolgirls. "What kind of Indian is your mother?" Ethel asked as she daintily pumped Zach's hand.

"A Shoshone."

"Why, that makes you half white and half redskin."

"I won't tell anyone if you won't," Zach quipped and was perplexed when the sisters laughed as if he were the wittiest person who'd ever lived.

"That's the spirit," Earnest Livingston remarked and Aunt Martha nodded.

Exactly what they were implying eluded Zach. He was going to ask the lawyer to explain but Harry clamped a calloused hand on his while giving his shoulder a squeeze that could crush rock.

"I'm real pleased to meet you, Zachary. If Louisa likes you, that's good enough for me. She and I have been close since we were barely out of diapers."

For lack of anything better to say, Zach replied, "Didn't I hear tell you work in a mill back in Ohio?"

"I sure do." Harry grinned, with an uneasy glance at his father. "It doesn't pay as much as some jobs do, but I like it. My boss says I do the work of two men, I'm so strong."

Zach believed it. He took an instinctive liking to the young man. "Some day you'll have to visit Lou and me in the mountains. I think you'd like it up there."

"I'd love to," Harry said. "I've heard all sorts of stories. Is it true there are bears as big as cabins? And that there are more buffalo then there are blades of grass?"

"My pa killed a grizzly once that was twelve feet high

at the shoulder. Or so my Uncle Shakespeare claims but he's mighty partial to tall tales. That's the biggest one I ever heard of." Zach noticed Martha's eyes narrow. "The Indians called it the Father of All Bears."

"Tell me more about life in the mountains," Harry coaxed.

Earnest put a hand on his son's shoulder. "Perhaps later, Harold. Right now we have a much more important subject to discuss. Louisa's engagement."

"Most definitely," Aunt Martha echoed. "I want to hear all about it."

Lou was relieved everything was going so well. Her relatives didn't dislike Zach just because of his mixed parentage, as so many whites did. "If it's all the same to you, Aunt Martha, could we do it later? Mr. Goujon has graciously invited us to stay here at the estate, and Zach and I must go into the city to fetch our belongings from Adam Tyler's. It shouldn't take more than an hour."

Earnest Livingston's height seemed to increase several inches. "Am I to infer the two of you have been—"

"Don't be such a bore, Earnest," Aunt Martha quickly said. "Make yourself useful. I'm going with Louisa and her fiancé. You stay and comfort poor Thomas. He's taking the death of his brother quite hard."

"But—"

"Are you disputing me?" Martha asked in a tone that implied it was unwise to do so.

"Never," Earnest answered, and, with a nod at Zach and Lou, he walked over to the chair where Thomas Clark, deeply despondent, sat with his elbows on his knees and his chin in his hands.

"May we tag along?" Ethel inquired.

"And me," Harry said.

Aunt Martha wagged a finger. "No on both counts. Louisa and I have a lot of catching up to do. The three of you can take a stroll in the gardens or go horseback riding or whatever strikes your fancy."

73

David Thompson

Suddenly Racine was there, bowing and smiling. "If I may be so bold, Madam Livingston. Monsieur Goujon has put me at your complete disposal, and it would be my supreme honor to escort these two lovely ladies—and Monsieur Clark, here, also, of course—to my master's lily ponds. They would enjoy the walk. The ducks and goldfish can be most entertaining."

"You'll be their chaperone, is that it?" Aunt Martha said. "And who will chaperone you?"

"Why would I need one, madame?" Racine asked, sounding mildly offended.

"Oh, please. It's not as if I fell out of the sky with the last cloudburst. I've seen how you look at my niece Gladys."

Lou glanced at her cousin, whose sheepish countenance confirmed Martha's statement. Now Lou better understood the Cajun's flattering comments.

Racine was too flustered to respond but someone else came to his rescue.

"Perhaps we would qualify as suitable chaperones," Adam Tyler intervened, Celeste Goujon at his side. "We were planning on taking a stroll ourselves."

Celeste added, "I assure you, madame, your nieces will be perfectly safe. I'll have a couple of servant girls attend us every step of the way."

"I suppose that would be suitable enough," Aunt Martha reluctantly conceded. Satisfied, she rested a hand on Louisa and another on Zach and steered them toward the doorway. "Let's be off, shall we? I can't wait to hear all about how the two of you met and became engaged. Leaving nothing out. I want every little detail." She laughed merrily.

Zach didn't share her enthusiasm. He couldn't help but wonder why Martha wasn't as upset at learning of Zeb's death as Thomas was. Zeb had been married to her sister, after all. But since Lou didn't appear particularly bothered by it, Zach let himself be ushered along the plush hall. For some reason, just at that juncture a saying common among whites rose unbidden in his mind. He couldn't recall all of it, but it was something about a lamb and slaughter.

Chapter Six

Worrying was a waste of energy and emotion. A person could get all wrought up over something or other, they could fret themselves half to death in the firm belief dire calamity was sure to befall, only to find out all their worrying had been for naught when nothing bad happened.

Zachary King had about turned himself into a nervous wreck. He was so concerned over the impression he'd make on his beloved's relatives, he was so anxious over whether they would accept him with open arms or reject him, that he'd felt physically queasy several times when they arrived and during the subsequent carriage ride into St. Louis with Aunt Martha.

Hours later, in the cool of the evening, the lush countryside shrouded in thickening twilight, Zach was perched in a comfortable chair at the rear of the Goujon mansion, sipping lemonade a maid had brought him and grinning at his silliness.

The ride into the city had gone extremely well. Aunt Martha had listened to Lou's account of how Zach and her met, asking questions now and then but generally keeping her own counsel. By the time they reached Adam Tyler's, Martha had learned all there was of importance. Zach had waited with bated breath for her reaction.

It came in the form of a hug and a cheery declaration. "Land sakes! It just tickles me, Louisa, to know you've found the love of your life, as you call him. I'm glad you brought him to meet us, more glad than you'll ever know."

To Zach, Martha said, "As for you, young man, I'll have you know you're marrying one of the sweetest, kindest girls who ever lived. I expect you to take real good care of her."

Zach had vowed he would, and from that moment on, Aunt Martha and him were the best of friends. On the carriage ride back to the plantation Martha plied him with a thousand questions about his father and mother, about the Shoshones, and about life in the wilderness in general. Before going off with Lou to tidy up for supper, Martha had given him another hug and remarked what a fine couple they made.

Now, smiling, Zach took a sip of lemonade, then said aloud, "I'm the biggest chucklehead who ever lived."

"You don't say?" Earnest Livingston sank into the white wicker chair beside his, the lawyer's thin lips curled upward in what, on him, amounted to a grin.

Flustered, Zach sat up. "I was talking to myself," he said lamely. "It's a habit. From being in the deep woods so much, I reckon."

"I talk to myself all the time, and I've never been in the deep woods," Earnest said. "Of course, I've trained myself not to do it around Martha. A man can get into no end of trouble with one slip of the tongue." He winked good-naturedly.

Zach didn't know what to say. He was flabbergasted by the lawyer's drastic change in manner and attitude.

As if reading Zach's thoughts, Earnest said, "I've just had a long talk with my wife. She told me how pleased she is about Louisa and you, how overjoyed she is to have you become part of our family." Earnest held out his hand. "So permit me extend my sincere congratulations."

Stupefied, Zach shook.

"From here on out, I want you to consider me just as much your uncle as Louisa does. Don't feel shy about asking my help or advice. People tend to treat lawyers like lepers, but I'm not without my redeeming qualities."

"Yes, sir." Zach almost pinched himself to verify his turn of fortune. *They were accepting him! They were honestly and truly accepting him as one of them!* It was too good to be true, his dream made real.

"This has turned into quite a trip," Earnest commented. "You and Louisa, Gladys and Racine."

"They're serious about each other?" Zach said to hold up his end of the conversation.

"Racine certainly is smitten. And Gladys can't stop talking about him." Earnest stretched out his long legs and crossed them at the ankles. "Racine, though, has another ten years of indentured servitude ahead of him. It would be terribly rough on them until he's legally free to live as he wants."

"You don't mind that's he indentured to Mr. Goujon?" Somehow, Zach had gotten the impression Earnest didn't think highly of servants—or half-breeds, either.

"Why should I mind? I'm a lawyer, not a judge. Lawyers don't sit in judgement on others. We mold the law to best suit justice." Earnest folded his hands behind his head. "All I want is what's best for everyone. If it's best for Lou to wed you, so be it. If it's best for Thomas's daughter to take up with Racine, so be it."

"What does Thomas think?"

"He's too heartbroken over the death of his brother to

give Gladys's romantic longings the attention it deserves. Even so, Tom has always been much more lenient with his daughters than I ever was with Harry. Too lenient, if you ask me. A parent should be caring but firm."

"My pa is that way."

"Is he indeed? Excellent. Parenting isn't easy. It's not a responsibility to be taken lightly. Parents must make hard decisions on occasion, decisions our offspring resent. Yet it is crucial we do what is right for them, whether they agree or not."

Zach couldn't think of anything suitable to say so he said the first thing that popped into his head. "I hear you were disappointed your son couldn't follow in your footsteps."

Earnest glanced around sharply, then quickly glanced away. "Someone has been talking out of turn, have they? Well, it's no secret. Yes, my fondest wish once was that my son would become a lawyer. I had his future all mapped out practically from the day he was born. Law school, the bar, legal practice, maybe a political career. But it wasn't meant to be."

"Harry is a fine man," Zach said. "You should be proud."

"He's friendly and outgoing and honest, I'll grant you that," Earnest said. "Oh, don't take me wrong. I've long since come to terms with the disappointment. I realize you can't make a silk purse out of a sow's ear. Or a president out of a bump—" Earnest caught himself. "Or a president out of a mill worker."

"It isn't so much the work we do as how we do it. That's what my pa always says."

Earnest faced him. "I'm curious. Your father, his name is Nate, correct? He's quite content being a mountain man? He has no higher aspirations?"

"He's happy being who he is, yes. He told me once that if happiness was gold, he'd be the richest man in the world."

The lawyer was quiet a minute. "I envy him, then. I can't

recall a single day in my whole life when I've been really happy. Content, perhaps. But never happy."

Out of the mansion came Jacques Goujon, Auguste, and George Milhouse. The old trapper and the younger Goujon had become inseparable, Milhouse regaling Auguste with tales of the high country from the days when trapping was in its infancy.

"—tribes have their womenfolk wear chastity belts," the grizzled mountaineer was saying. "The Cheyennes, for instance. Trifle with one of their unmarried females, and you'll be bristlin' with enough arrows to turn you into a porcupine."

Earnest snickered and said so only Zach could hear, "Is that all he ever talks about? Women?"

Jacques approached, all smiles. "Gentlemen! Supper will be served in about five minutes. If you would attend me, we will repair to the dining room."

Rising, Zach saw Adam Tyler and Celeste strolling in the gardens. They walked so close to one another, they were constantly brushing arms. Jacques called to her, and she waved and headed back.

"Your daughter and that gambler," Earnest addressed the patriarch. "I take it you approve?"

"Why wouldn't I, Monsieur Livingston?" Jacques said. "Adam Tyler is a man of great integrity."

"He makes his living at cards."

"So? You make it sound despicable, but gambling is an old and honorable profession." Jacques gestured. "Besides, my daughter hasn't been this cheerful in ages. After months and months of crying herself to sleep, she has a newfound zest for life. And I daresay, so does Monsieur Tyler."

"Romance is in the air, *non?*" Auguste bantered. "Next thing you know, I will fall in love with one of the maids."

"You do and I will shoot you," Jacques said, much more somberly than was warranted.

Zach trailed the older men indoors. He failed to see why it was all right for Celeste to show interest in a gambler but not all right for Auguste to show interest in a maid. Was a maid somehow less worthy? The logic eluded him.

Shaking his head, Zach didn't give it any further thought. So long as Lou's kin were pleased with him, that was all that mattered. He grinned at how silly he had been earlier, at how worked up he had become over nothing. He would never do that again.

As they negotiated the maze of corridors, an odd incident occurred. They were passing a junction and Zach idly glanced to his right. Just as he did, Aunt Martha and Racine appeared at the far end. Zach had started to look away, so it was possible Martha didn't realize he had spotted them. Even so, her next act was decidedly peculiar, for she grabbed Racine's arm and hauled him back around the corner, out of sight.

Zach took several more strides, then halted. He couldn't rightly say what prompted him to sidle to the corner and peek around it. Aunt Martha and Racine had reappeared and were coming toward him, Martha talking in a low voice, the Cajun listening with his head bowed. Zach tried to hear what she was saying but it wasn't until they were almost on top of him that he could.

"—settled, then. You scratch my back and I'll scratch yours. Agreed?"

"*Oui,* madame. Although, truth to tell, my heart is not in it."

"Think of the reward in store for you. I'll help you, but only if you help me kill two birds with one stone."

"You are full of platitudes, Madame Clark."

"Full of what?"

Zach was about to step into the open, then act as innocent as a newborn at running into them. But a loud voice behind him spoiled his plan.

"Monsieur King! My father sent me to find you. We feared you had become lost." Auguste Goujon, smiling in his usual friendly way, was coming up the hall.

*   *   *

Zach moved to the middle a split second before Aunt Martha and Racine reached the junction. "There you are," he said to give the impression he had been searching for them. "We're about to sit down to eat."

Aunt Martha glanced at Auguste, then at Zach. "I know. Mr. Racine is escorting me since I can't find my husband anywhere."

"He is up ahead, madame," Auguste said, stepping aside for her to go by. "I shall reunite the two of you in no time."

"We'll follow you," Aunt Martha said.

The suggestion was unthinkable to Auguste. "Ladies first, always, Madame Clark. Above all else, my father raised me to be a gentleman."

Once again Zach brought up the rear. He didn't know what to make of Aunt Martha's secretive behavior or the little he had overheard. Even more bewildering were his own antics. What compelled him to eavesdrop? Why had he treated them as potential enemies after Martha made it clear she was all in favor if his marriage to Louisa?

Zach blamed it on his warrior training, on his naturally suspicious nature. Despite the many hugs and fond wishes Martha had bestowed, he couldn't quite believe she was sincere. He persisted in thinking of her as a potential enemy when he should view her as a kindly ally.

Old habits were hard to break, Zach observed. As far as Aunt Martha's antics with the Cajun, there had to be a sound reason. The best way to find out was to march right up to her and ask, but Zach couldn't bring himself to do it. She'd think he was prying. And so long as she approved so heartily of Lou and him, he'd make a special point of walking on hawk's eggs around her.

Presently they came to the dining room. Zach took two steps in and stopped dead, astounded. He'd thought the parlor was huge but this new room dwarfed it. A polished hardwood floor stretched for hundreds of feet. Not one but *three* chandeliers adorned the high ceiling. The centerpiece a long mahogany table, although "long" was an inadequate description. It seemed to go on forever. There was enough wood in that table, Zach reflected, to build three whole cabins. No, make that four.

"You look a bit taken aback," Earnest Livingston remarked.

"I've just never seen a table before where the person at one end needs a telescope to see the person at the other end."

The lawyer's mouth quirked. "Yes, I find this mansion a tad intimidating myself. Martha and I are well-to-do, but we're nowhere near as rich as the Goujons. They're what people refer to as old money. Meaning they have more than they'll ever know what to do with."

"You sound as if you envy them."

"Any sane man would," Earnest said. "What husband worth his salt doesn't want to provide his family with the very best he can? Wealth and luxury are the earmarks of our success, of our station in this world. They're the measure of our worth as a man."

"Among my people, the measure of a warrior's worth is how many coup he's counted," Zach revealed.

"Your people? You consider yourself more Indian than white, then?"

Was it Zach's imagination, or did he detect thinly veiled scorn? "I'm as proud of my red blood as I am of my white blood." More so, in some regards, but the lawyer didn't need to know that. Only an idiot would rock a canoe when it was floating smoothly along.

"Really? Based on your previous comment earlier, I'd assumed differently."

Zach was trying to recall which comment when Louisa bounced over, took him by the arm, and led him to one side. She was positively radiant, sunnier than Zach had ever seen her.

"How are you holding up, darling?"

"Well enough. No one has tried to lift my scalp yet."

"I was serious," Lou said, chuckling. She had spent the

past half an hour with Ethel and Gladys, reliving their childhoods.

"So was I," Zach replied.

"You're such a worrywart," Lou scolded. "My aunt thinks you're wonderful, and all of them have been wishing the two of us well. I knew they would. They're great people."

"Do you think your aunt approves of Racine and Gladys?"

Louisa pivoted toward the table. Aunt Martha smiled and gave a little wave so Lou returned the favor. "I don't know. She hasn't come right out and spoken against it. Gladys likes Racine a lot but they wouldn't have much of a life together until his period of servitude is over."

Zach was struck by how much she sounded like Earnest. "If they care for each other, why should that matter?" Zach thought of Earnest's other comment, about wealth, and of the pleasure Lou took in the trappings of luxury. "Can I ask you a question?"

Lou had begun to steer him to their spot at the table but she stopped. "Anything. Anytime. Don't you know that?"

"Will you really be content to live out the rest of your days up in the mountains?"

"Why wouldn't I be?" Lou rejoined, hurt he would even ask. "I love you, silly goose. I'll be happy wherever we are."

"We'll never have a home like this, never be this rich."

"So?" Laughing, Lou kissed him on the cheek. "Honestly, you fret over the silliest stuff. It's you I want, not some big old mansion or a carriage fit for royalty." Amused, she drew up behind two empty chairs between those of Aunt Martha and Uncle Thomas. Many more chairs had gone unfilled than filled. Lou made a rough mental count and calculated there were seating arrangements for upward of seventy.

Another Cajun servant in a smart uniform materialized. Zach didn't much like having a man pull out his chair for him, but since none of the other men had made a fuss, he didn't, either.

Maids were hurrying back and forth from the kitchen, bearing tray after tray. The table filled with platters of venison, of quail, of beef, ham, and lamb. With bowls of potatoes, carrots, green beans, and corn on the cob heaped high. With bread and biscuits, butter and jam. The last time Zach had seen so much food was at a feast put on by a Shoshone chief for some visiting Flatheads and Nez Percé. There was enough to feed a village, much more than those present could eat, and he wondered if what was left uneaten would go to waste.

After everyone had sat down, Jacques Goujon rose to say grace. "We thank you, Lord, for the bounty of your blessing. We thank you also for the gift of our new friends. Watch over us and protect us all the days of our lives. Amen."

Zach noticed that Racine wasn't at the table. Evidently servants weren't permitted to dine with the family.

They were invited to help themselves. Zach loaded his plate with ham, a rarity in the Rockies, along with corn on the cob and a small mountain of potatoes covered with butter. He was about to take his first bite when Thomas Clark nudged his elbow.

"Why did they do it, Zachary? Can you explain that to me?"

"Sir?" Zach said.

Uncle Thomas had been up in his room since learning of his brother's death. His eyes were bloodshot from long weeping, his features pale and pinched. "Why did those filthy savages kill Zeb? He wasn't trying to harm them. He was minding his own business, making a living for himself and his daughter."

Zach lowered his fork.

"Why couldn't they leave him be? Tell me, please. You're part Indian. You must know how they think."

"They saw him as an enemy—"

David Thompson

"Why? Because he was white?"

"They'd have done the same to a Shoshone or a Crow or anyone else they caught trapping in their territory," Zach said. Which wasn't entirely true. It had been a hunting party, not a war party, and they had just happened to stumble on Zebulon's camp. Zeb had simply been in the wrong place at the wrong time.

A fierce glint came into Thomas's eyes. "What tribe did they belong to? I'd like to wipe out every last one."

"Gros Ventres, I think."

"You think?"

"I spoke to them, briefly, but they never said. Before I could find out, they tried to kill Lou and me. I had my hands full getting her out of there."

"Filthy, stinking savages," Uncle Thomas snarled. "We should exterminate the whole red race!" Rage seized him and he pounded the table so hard, nearby plates, glasses, and silverware bounced and clattered. "My brother never harmed a soul! Sure, he was always chasing one silly fantasy after another, but he was a good man at heart. A devoted husband, a caring father."

The room had been hushed by his outburst

"Please, Uncle Thomas," Louisa said. "No one misses him more than me, but this isn't the time or place."

"How can you say that? You should be torn up inside like I am. You should be filled with fury at the heathen devils who murdered him."

Once, briefly, right after Zeb died, Lou had felt the same. She'd hated Indians, hated them as she'd never hated anyone or anything. She'd believed they were everything their detractors painted them as: vicious, brutish barbarians. Then she'd met Zach and Zach's family, and it was like having cold water thrown in her face on a hot summer's day.

Yes, it was wrong of the Gros Ventres to slay her father for his plews. But only the warriors in the hunting party were to blame. Just as there were honorable, peaceable

86

whites, so were their honorable, peaceable red men. And just as there were whites who routinely killed, robbed, and raped, so were there red men who did the same. To put it in simpler terms, there were good whites and bad whites, good Indians and bad Indians.

"A few bad apples don't mean the whole tree should be chopped down," Lou quoted a favorite saying of her mother's.

"Is that all your father was to you? An apple?" Thomas Clark rose, a hand pressed to his brow. "Oh, that I should have lived to see this day."

Ethel and Gladys, seated on the other side of him, were portraits of anxiety. "Father, Louisa is right," Ethel said. "We loved Uncle Zeb as much as you, but we shouldn't show our grief in public. It's unbecoming."

"Do you think I care?" Thomas cried. Swaying like a reed in the wind, he gripped the table for support.

Zach was closest to the distraught man. He felt he should do something to help, but the only thing he could think of was to place his hand on the other's arm and say, "When I used to get upset, my ma always sent me outside to cool off. Maybe some fresh air would help. I'll go with you, if you'd like."

Thomas stared a moment at Zach's fingers, then his portly features contorted in raw spite and he angrily jerked away. "Don't touch me! Don't ever touch me! You're part Indian. That makes you little better than the bastards who slew Zeb."

"Enough!" Aunt Martha rose, indignant, her dress rustling as she swept past Lou and Zach. "You're childishness ends right this moment."

"But—" Thomas started to object.

Aunt Martha poked him in the chest. "Be quiet and listen," she commanded, as if he were a child who had misbehaved. "All of us grieve at your loss. All of us loved your brother. My sister most of all. She married him, shared his burdens, did all she could to be the best wife she could possibly be."

"What does—"

Once more Aunt Martha wouldn't let him finish. "When Marcy died, you didn't see me raging and ranting. I expect the same courtesy from you." She nodded at Zach. "This young man is no more to blame for Zebulon's death than I am. If you need to assign fault, lay it on Zeb himself."

"Now see here—"

"No, you see here. Zeb was never one to hold a steady job. He was always trying to make easy money, to get rich quick. That's what did him in. And the sooner you come to grips with it, the better off you'll be."

Uncle Thomas's portly face rippled in resentment. "I've heard quite enough, thank you very much. You'll excuse me if I don't stay." Wheeling, he stormed from the dining room, almost knocking over a servant who didn't get out of his way fast enough.

Aunt Martha surveyed the stunned onlookers. "That was his grief talking. Give him time. In another day or two he'll be fine."

Zach doubted it, but he did as everyone else was doing and resumed eating. He wasn't very hungry, though. The outburst had ruined his appetite. Once again bigotry had reared it ugly head. Granted, Thomas Clark had an excuse, but that didn't make the insult any more bearable. He ate half the ham and one piece of corn on the cob, then poked at his potatoes.

Little was said. Their merry bubble had been punctured, the mood spoiled. Once the meal was over, Celeste asked the women to join her in the sitting room. Jacques invited the men to share a cigar in his study.

Zach declined. He wanted some time to himself, to think. He grinned and waved to Lou as she flitted out with the other ladies, then he ambled to the rear of the mansion and stepped out into the muggy night. Under a canopy of stars the estate lay quiet. Restless, he walked to a tall weeping willow and leaned against the trunk.

Off in the darkness something moved. Zach spied a figure in the shadows and thought it might be a servant. "Who's there?" he asked.

The answer came in the form of dully glittering steel as a dagger flashed out of the gloom, streaking directly at Zach's heart.

Chapter Seven

Several years ago, on a crisp Autumn night in the high country, Zachary King had sat in the lodge of a famed Shoshone warrior known as Touch the Clouds. The huge warrior was widely acknowledged as the most formidable in the entire tribe, and Zach had come to him for instruction in the finer points of the arts of war.

A low fire crackled, filling the lodge with welcome warmth. Smoke rose in thin tendrils to vanish out the vent at the top. To one side the great warrior's wife and daughters were huddled, talking softly among themselves.

"A warrior must possess three traits above all else," Touch the Clouds had mentioned. "You must always be alert, Stalking Coyote. By alert, I mean you must be aware of all that goes on around you at all times. You must note all the little things most people miss. How the horses act when you are in camp. How the birds and animals act when

90

you are in the woods. The cry of an angry squirrel might be all that saves you from hidden enemies."

"What else?" Zach asked.

"A warrior must always be ready to kill. Not just have a weapon handy, for that is something you should do without thinking, like putting on your leggings or moccasins. You must go one step further. You must be mentally prepared to kill at any moment. Some men will not or can not do this. They go on raids to count coup, but once the raids are done, they go back to their peaceful way of living with no thought to killing." Touch the Clouds had tilted his great head to peer up through the vent. "An exceptional warrior, even in the safety of his own village or the comfort of his own lodge, is always ready to slay enemies. It does not matter where you are or what you are doing."

Zach had pondered the advice a while, then said, "What else?"

"You must control your fear and not let it control you."

"A true warrior is never afraid," Zach declared, irritated that Touch the Clouds would think so poorly of him.

"Is that so?" The huge Shoshone had chuckled. "I must not be a true warrior, then, for I have often been afraid. Remember that time the silver grizzly attacked me in the foothills? And when the Sioux war party cut me off from the rest of our raiding party? Many more times, besides."

"You're just saying that to make me think it is all right to be scared. But I know better."

"I do not speak with two tongues."

Zach had inadvertently accused Touch the Clouds of being a liar. He hastily apologized, adding, "I will take your word for it. But I have yet to feel the deep, gnawing fear some say they have. You will never catch me freezing in battle as they have done."

"No man can predict the future." The venerable warrior pondered for a few moments, then said, "Fear is like lightning, my young friend. It strikes out of nowhere when we least expect. The best we can do is recognize it for what it is and wipe it from our minds, much as we wipe out our tracks when we do not want to be followed."

"It should not be very difficult," Zach asserted.

"I thought the same when I had seen as many winters as you have. But with age comes experience, with experience, wisdom. If fear were easy to control, men would not dread it so."

Among the Shoshones and other tribes, cowardice was the shame of all shames. Men who lacked courage were looked down on; among the Crows, they were relegated to do women's work. Since their fellows could not count on them in the heat of a frenzied fight, they were not permitted to go on raids until they had proven themselves.

So it was understandable that young warriors dreaded showing fear. Zach had Shoshone friends his age who worried constantly that they would not live up to what was expected of them. Zach preferred not to dwell on it. There was an old saying among the whites: "Out of sight, out of mind." He liked to rephrase it as "Out of mind, out of body." If he didn't think about fear, fear couldn't have an effect.

Touch the Clouds had gone on. "When you feel fear, concentrate on what you are doing and it will go away. If you are being charged by a buffalo, concentrate on the buffalo. If an enemy is upon you, concentrate on the enemy. Fix your thoughts on what causes the fear, not on the fear itself, and you will survive."

Now the giant warrior's words were put to the test.

The instant Zach saw the dagger streaking toward him, fleeting fear erupted. But he didn't freeze, he didn't panic. His reflexes took over as he focused on the dully shimmering steel. Automatically he jerked aside. The cold blade thirsting for his warm blood thudded into the trunk of the willow instead. It all happened with such incredible swiftness that if an onlooker had blinked, they would have missed it.

Zach pivoted, drawing one of his flintlocks as he rotated

and fixing a bead on the shadowy figure, but the person took flight toward the east end of the mansion. Zach gave chase, pumping his legs furiously, his mind racing faster than his feet. Who had tried to kill him? he wondered. And why?

The figure veered toward the magnificent gardens the Goujons's maintained, covering many acres. Zach angled to cut him off but the assassin had too much of a lead. Flying into a gap in the neatly trimmed hedge, the figure disappeared.

In seconds Zach plunged through the opening, only to draw up in baffled consternation. Not one but three trails diverged—to the right, to the left, and one to the east. There was no telling which the would-be killer had taken. Zach listened but heard only the wind and distant voices from the direction of the cabins the slaves lived in. Bending, he sought tracks. In the near-total darkness, finding any was impossible.

Zach considered using a lantern, but by the time he returned with one, the assassin would be long gone. Severely disappointed, he wedged the flintlock under his belt to the left of the big buckle and walked back to the willow. The dagger was buried almost to the hilt. Whoever had thrown it was immensely strong. Gripping it with both hands, Zach braced a foot against the bole and pulled. A lot of tugging later, he wrenched the weapon free.

Going indoors, Zach examined it. The blade was double-edged, about six inches long, the hilt solid ivory inset with sparkling gems. Zach examined them, his mind churning anew. A dagger like this one cost a small fortune. Only someone with substantial wealth could afford it, and the only people Zach knew who possessed that much money were his hosts. He couldn't believe it was one of the Goujons, though. They had no cause to want him dead.

None that he knew of, anyway.

If not them, then who? That was the crucial question. No one had so much as glanced at Zach crosswise all day, with

93

the exception of Thomas Clark. Sliding the dagger into an inner pocket, Zach started to go in search of Lou. The click of the latch in the outside door brought him around in a crouch, his hands diving to his pistols.

The portly form of Thomas Clark filled the doorway. "You!" he blurted, acting surprised. "Is the meal over, then?"

"It's been over for some time," Zach said icily. He wanted to blow out the man's wick then and there.

Uncle Thomas glanced at Zach's waist. "What's wrong? Why do you have your hands on your guns?"

"I suppose you have a good excuse for being outside?" Zach challenged.

"What does that have to do with anything?" Uncle Thomas said. "For your information, I was taking your advice. I needed to clear my head after my outburst so I went out for some fresh air."

"That's all you did?"

"What else? I went for a stroll in the gardens." Uncle Thomas shut the door. "I really must apologize for my atrocious behavior. I'm afraid my grief over Zeb got the better of me. Can you ever find it in your heart to forgive me?"

Zach slowly straightened. The man seemed sincere, yet if it hadn't been Thomas who tried to kill him, then who? "Did you see anyone else while you were out there?"

"Not a soul, although I did hear someone go running off down a different path as I was making my way back. Or maybe it was one of those big dogs the Goujons have. Why?"

Confused, Zach didn't answer. Part of him desired to put holes in Clark or pound the man into the floor. Yet the more Zach though about it, the more preposterous it was that Uncle Thomas had been the one who tried to murder him. Whoever threw the dagger was highly skilled at hurling bladed weapons, a skill Zach doubted Clark possessed. "Ever owned a knife?"

"What kind of question is that? I had a folding knife

when I was little, but that's about it. I'm a businessman, not a hunter." Uncle Thomas extended his hand. "How about it? No hard feelings over my temper tantrum?"

Against his better judgement, Zach shook.

"Thank you. I truly am sorry." Uncle Thomas clapped Zach on the shoulder, then walked off.

For a long time Zach stood there, pondering. The Goujons, the Livingstons, and the two Clark girls had all treated him decently. None seemed to care he wasn't white or shown resentment at his engagement to Lou.

Whoever was to blame, one fact was clear; They would probably try again.

In a plush sitting room on the second floor Louisa was listening to Aunt Martha relate the hardships of overland travel from Ohio to St. Louis.

"—coaches were positively horrid. They bounced and swayed at every tiny bump and rut. Dust was a constant problem, caking our clothes, our hair. And on occasion swarms of insects flew in the windows, even when we had the flaps down. It was awful."

"I didn't mind the swaying and bouncing so much," Ethel said. "It made me sleepy, like rocking in a rocking chair."

Gladys sniffed. "All I really minded was the foul language and atrocious manners of some of the people we met along the way. It became worse the farther west we traveled. Why, at one stop, a man barreled right past me and into a shop without so much as bothering to hold the door."

Celeste Goujon had contributed little during the past hour. Most of the time she gazed rather wistfully out a window. Now she bestirred herself to say, "Where life is rough, so are the people. My father took it into his head once to hunt buffalo. This was back when my mother was still alive. We traveled to Fort Leavenworth and from there a short distance out on the prairie."

"Wasn't that dangerous?" Gladys asked. "What about Indians?" She glanced at Lou. "I mean, hostile Indians?"

"We had an army escort," Celeste said, "but it was still an ordeal. We could not bathe, we could not even wash our hair. We lived in small tents, with only the barest of necessities. The soldiers often employed crude and vulgar language within our hearing. Not on purpose, mind you, but it was upsetting nonetheless."

"You poor dear," Aunt Martha said.

"We ate well but the fare was simple. Venison, rabbit, once or twice some elk meat. My father and my brother loved it. They rode off every morning with our scout and some of the troopers to hunt, leaving my mother and me to fend for ourselves. There was little to do other than read and play cards. I was never so bored in my life." Celeste paused. "I am a creature of the city. I love the theater, the concerts, the gala balls. Give me culture over frontier existence any day."

Lou recalled the trophies mounted in the hall. "Did your pa get his buffalo?"

"Yes, he shot a big bull. Its head hangs over his bed so he can admire it every night. He was quite proud, *mon pere.* For him it was grand excitement. The next summer he wanted to go back. Thankfully, my mother refused. His feelings were hurt but she was not feeling well so he had to honor her wishes."

Aunt Martha chuckled. "That's a man for you. They never do anything unless we twist their arm. Or kick them out of bed until they comes to their senses."

"Aunt Martha!" Gladys declared. "That's indecent."

"But it's the truth, child, as you'll learn soon enough. Most men have the brains of a mule and the stubbornness to match. Why the good Lord saw fit to create them that way, I'll never know. But you can talk yourself blue in the face and there's no getting through to them. The best you can hope for is to hook a man who worships the ground you walk on so he'll bend over backwards to please you."

"I do not share your low opinion of men, Madame

Clark," Celeste said. "My husband, Philippe, was almost all a woman could ask for."

"Don't get me wrong, dearie," Aunt Martha said. "I'm not saying all males are lost causes. Maybe ten percent are worth the bother. My Earnest, for example, is as polite as can be. And he has the good sense not to argue with me when I'm right, which is all the time."

They shared a laugh, then Gladys beckoned to the maid, who promptly refilled her tea cup. "I don't care how bad you make them sound. I know that somewhere in this world is the perfect man for me."

"Mr. Racine?" Aunt Martha said, and when her niece flushed, Martha cackled. "Don't get your dander up, girl. I wasn't poking fun. Truth is, I like him. He's a gentleman, through and through." She took a sip of her own tea. "Of course, there's the little matter of his being indentured. That's a serious obstacle if you're considering him as a potential husband."

"Husband!" Gladys exclaimed. "Land sakes! Where did you ever get that silly idea? I like him, yes, but not enough to marry him."

Aunt Martha smiled. "A fling, is it? Well, just so you don't get carried away. But it's nice to know you have a good head on your shoulders. You must have Livingston blood in you."

Lou's aunt and cousins tittered, but Lou was appalled. It stunned her to learn Gladys was leading Racine on. The Cajun's affection was sincere, and Lou thought it wrong of her cousin to mislead him. Whether he was an indentured servant or not was irrelevant. Evidently she wasn't the only one who thought so.

"If you do not care for Monsieur Racine," Celeste said to Gladys, "you should tell him, Mademoiselle Clark. A lady never deceives a gentleman about her intentions."

"Perish forbid," Aunt Martha said. "Don't worry, Celeste. I'll see to it my niece doesn't step out of line."

"I hope so, Madame Clark," Celeste responded. "Racine

is more than a servant to me. He is a trusted friend. I would take it personally were Gladys to hurt him."

"Never fear. We'll do what's right," Aunt Martha pledged.

The one aspect of staying at the Goujon plantation Zach liked least was having his room so far from his betrothed's. Louisa was at the south end; he was at the north.

At his folks's cabin they had slept in the same room—Zach on one side, Lou and his sister, Evelyn, on the other. Often he woke up in the middle of the night and watched Louisa sleep, drinking in the sight of her beauty, dazzled by his good fortune in winning her heart.

At Adam Tyler's, Lou had been just down the hall. Zach got up once or twice a night and tiptoed down it to stand in front of her bedroom door and listen to her breathing. Sometimes he would touch the door gently, as if touching her, then go back to the living room and Milhouse's nonstop snoring.

Now, lying in a soft down bed on the third floor of the mansion, Zach heard an owl voice the eternal query of its kind from a stand of maples close by. He found himself missing Lou terribly and wishing they could be alone for a while. It was important he tell her about the attempt on his life.

They had seen each other briefly before turning in. Zach had joined the other men in Jacques's study, the room so thick with cigar smoke he'd barely been able to breathe. Uncle Thomas was there and he'd apologized again, in public, for his "atrocious antics" at supper, as he described them.

Later, by prearrangement, the men had joined the women in the parlor. Zach longed to be alone with Louisa but someone was always with her. It wasn't until shortly before ten that he finally got her to himself for a few moments.

"I've missed you," Lou said, pecking his cheek. "Since we got here we've hardly had two minutes alone."

"We need to talk," Zach replied.

"About what?"

Before Zach could answer, Aunt Martha breezed over and looped her arm through Louisa's.

"Here you are! It's almost ten. Time for bed, my galli-vanting little niece. The two of you can make cow's eyes at each other another time."

"But—" Lou tried to protest.

"Now, now, young lady," Aunt Martha said. "It's been a busy day. We all need a good night's sleep. Tomorrow you lovebirds can spend hours together."

Zach could tell Lou hadn't liked it, but she had gone off with her aunt, leaving him to simmer with resentment until Jules appeared to guide him to his bedchamber. Hours spent tossing and turning had done little to improve his disposi-tion.

It had been a mistake to accept Jacques's invitation, Zach decided. He'd much rather have stayed at Adam Tyler's, where Lou and he enjoyed a measure of privacy when they needed it.

Zach had spoken to the gambler before Adam headed back into the city. They'd been waiting on the marble steps for the carriage to roll around when Adam bent toward him and asked, "Isn't she magnificent?"

"Celeste?"

"Who else? Lou's Aunt Martha?"

Zach grinned. "I've noticed that you like Celeste a lot."

"She reminds me of my beloved Mary. Her hair, her eyes, even her face. It's as if Mary has come back to life."

"She's not Mary, though," Zach had remarked, out of concern his friend was attracted to Celeste Goujon for the wrong reason.

"Do you think I don't know that? She's her own woman. I'll never make the mistake of confusing the two." The gambler had pulled his hat brim lower. "Just between the two of us, son, I intend to court her. She's filled me with a new zest for life. I haven't felt like this since I was sixteen. I feel so"—he paused as if searching for the right word—"alive."

"I'm glad for you, Adam."

"Thank you. And if things work out as I pray they do, I won't forget I owe all my happiness to you."

"Me?" Zach said. "What did I do?"

"Meeting you directly led to my meeting Celeste. If I hadn't come to your aid when you were fighting those rivermen, I might never have encountered her." Adam squeezed Zach's hand. "I'm forever in your debt. You have only to say the word and you can count on me for anything."

"There's no need."

"Nonsense." The carriage arrived and Adam bounded down the steps, laughing to himself. He jumped into the air and yipped, startling the driver, then yanked open the door. Glancing up, he stressed, "Anything, son." After he climbed in, the driver cracked the whip and the team surged forward.

Thinking of it now, Zach smiled. He had experienced the same exuberant glee when he met Louisa. The night they'd shared their first kiss had been one of the greatest of his whole life. His body had tingled for hours afterward, and every step he took felt as if he were floating on air.

Sitting up, Zach ran a hand across his forehead. He was too restless to sleep. Trying was a waste of time. Stepping to the window, he opened it to admit cool air and leaned on the sill.

The owl no longer hooted but the night was alive with other sounds: the musical chirp of crickets, the throaty croak of frogs, the strident cries of night birds. From off toward the lowland swamp came a faint, raspy snarl, the trademark of a prowling cougar.

Jacques Goujon had advised his guests to fight shy of the treacherous swampland. It abutted the estate to the north, mile after mile of marshy lowland adjacent to the Mississippi, stretching into the heart of the unknown. Some of the Cajuns, Jacques revealed, had penetrated a short way, but no one knew what lay in its shadowed depths. No one cared to know. There were rumors of creatures better left alone, of giant snakes and what Jacques called a three-toed skunk ape.

Zach would love to take his rifle and a parfleche full of jerky and explore the swamp but he was loathe to leave Louisa alone. Reaching up to close the window, he detected movement below, near the stable. The stable door opened and closed. After a few moments a soft glow rimmed the broad double doors. Someone had lit a lantern.

It was unusually late for the stablehands to be working. Curious, Zach stayed where he was. Soon a figure materialized, moving rapidly from the mansion toward the double doors. The figure rapped twice, and the person who had lit the lantern swung a door open just wide enough to admit them.

For a second the silhouette of a dress was outlined in the opening. The door closed too soon, however, for Zach to identify who wore it. But he would like to find out. Lowering the window, he sat on the bed and was about to don the shoes Adam had given him when he changed his mind. On an impulse he hurriedly undressed from head to toe. Then, from one of several beaded parfleches in the closet, he removed his folded buckskins and moccasins.

Slipping into them was like slipping into his own skin. Zach had forgotten how natural it felt to wear them, how comfortable they were. Smiling to himself, he attached the bowie's sheath to his wide, leather belt, strapped the belt around his waist, and wedged both of his pistols under it. He thought about taking the Hawken but opted to leave it behind. He'd have some explaining to do if anyone spotted him going about armed with a rifle. Besides which, in the dark, at close range, the flintlocks were just as reliable.

Cracking the door, Zach insured the dark hallway was empty. He slipped out, eased the door shut, and padded to the stairs. As silently as a specter, he descended. As he neared the second-floor landing he heard a cough and stopped.

Someone was shuffling up the stairs. Zach crouched beside the railing, his right hand on the bowie's smooth hilt. Flickering light appeared. Then a candleholder and a burning candle, held aloft by a pudgy hand. Into view stepped Uncle Thomas, attired in a striped nightshirt and a matching cap.

Zach wondered why Clark was abroad so late. A thick slab of bread and meat in Uncle Thomas's other hand testified to a nightly ritual that explained why the man was so portly. Zach ducked low.

Uncle Thomas came to the landing and paused to take a huge bite. Smacking his lips, he plodded off, his cap drooping over an ear.

Straightening, Zach continued down. Both Uncle Thomas and Uncle Earnest had rooms on the second floor. Zach hadn't given it much thought, but now it struck him as strange that he was the only one on the third floor. He didn't think the Goujons had a prejudiced bone in their body, so why had they placed him so far from everyone else?

Dismissing the speculation with a shake of his head, Zach concentrated on what he was doing. At the bottom he pressed an ear to the outer door. Hearing nothing out of the ordinary, he inched it open, bent at the waist, and angled to the right so his back was to the outer wall.

The lantern in the stable was still lit.

Zach dropped onto his hands and knees and scanned the yard from end to end. It appeared deserted. He felt safe in rising and racing across the grassy tract between the mansion and the outbuildings. Through the double doors wafted muffled voices, those of a woman and man. In order to hear better and learn who they were, Zach gripped the edge of the right-hand door to pull it open a fraction. Suddenly he froze.

Behind him something had growled.

Chapter Eight

Louisa May Clark couldn't sleep. She was too restless. Exactly why was difficult for her to say, unless it had something to do with her uncle's outburst at supper. Everything else had gone so well she had no cause to be upset.

For the umpteenth time, Lou rolled from one side to the other and hiked the blanket to her chin. She closed her eyes, willing herself to relax. Her body obeyed, the tension draining away like water from a sieve, but her mind continued to gallop along pell-mell. She couldn't stop thinking about Zach. They'd only been separated a short while, but she missed him tremendously.

Rolling onto her back, Lou stared at the ceiling. She remembered him saying they needed to talk, remembered her aunt breaking them apart. He'd had a hurt look on his face, which at the time she'd chalked up to his being irritated at Aunt Martha. Now she had second thoughts. Maybe it had been something important.

Abruptly, Lou sat up and slid off the bed. Taking her heavy robe from the copper hook on the wall, she bundled herself in it, then put on her slippers. Her aunt would frown on what she was about to do, but that was too bad. Lou wanted—no, she *needed*—to see Zach, and she was going to see him, come hades or high water.

The hall was empty. Lou was almost to the head of the main stairs when it dawned on her she didn't know which room Zach was in. Frustrated, she stamped her foot, then glanced back down the hall, afraid someone had heard.

Since she was already up and thirsty, Lou went downstairs and headed for the kitchen. She was mildly surprised to see a lamp was on, even more surprised when she saw who was seated at the table, sipping tea. "Celeste?"

The distaff Goujon wore a luxurious black silken robe over her nightclothes. It contrasted sharply with her lustrous golden hair, which was done up in a ponytail. Her makeup had been removed, her face scrubbed clean, but nothing could detract from her natural stunning beauty. "Mademoiselle Clark. You can not sleep either?"

"No," Lou admitted, moving to the stove. "Must be all that ham I ate. Mind if I help myself?"

"Be my guest, mademoiselle."

"Quit with the fancy French talk, will you?" Lou said. "It's Louisa. Or Lou. You ought to know better by now."

"I am most sorry."

Lou sat across from her. They stared at one another in uncomfortable silence until Celeste said something that shocked Lou silly.

"If you do not mind my saying so, you are quite attractive. Your Zachary is very fortunate."

"Let me get this straight. *You* think *I'm* pretty?"

"*Oui.* You have an ambience, an air about you. Not many do. Your cousins, Ethel and Gladys, for instance. They are charming in their ordinary way but they lack your dynamic essence."

Lou wasn't quite sure what all of that meant, but she was flattered, nonetheless. "It's sweet of you to say, even if you are joshing."

"We are not the only insomniacs," Celeste said. "Your uncle Thomas was here a while ago, in need of food."

"Has Zach been down?" Lou asked hopefully.

"No, he has not." Celeste downed the rest of her tea in two gulps and set the china cup on a matching saucer. "Anyone with eyes can see the two of you are greatly in love. I envy you. After my husband, Phillipe, died, I thought I would never know love again. Yet now—"

"Adam Tyler is a fine man. You could do worse."

"But it has only been a year since Phillipe passed on. I worry I am drawn to Monsieur Tyler more out of loneliness than affection. The human heart can be so fickle."

"I wouldn't know. I've never been in love before."

"Ah." Celeste smiled indulgently. "To be so young, so innocent. When you are my age, you view the world differently. We flatter ourselves the years make us wise but all they really make us is jaded."

Lou was totally at a loss. "Wasn't your marriage a happy one?"

"Oh, *oui*. It was as joyous as any union can be. Still, certain elements were lacking. Philippe was not very romantic, while I am. When we were younger I did not mind so much, but as the years passed I often yearned for him to be more considerate. I felt profound guilt when he died, as if my yearning had somehow killed him."

"That's silly."

"In my head I agree. In my heart, well—" Celeste frowned. "It was a riding accident, you see. Philippe was a superb horseman and liked to show off his skill. One morning when I was on the balcony having breakfast, he rode by and waved to me. Then he tried to jump a stone fence he had jumped many times before. But his horse stumbled, throwing Phillipe, breaking his neck."

"And you blame yourself?"

"I know it is ludicrous, my young friend. But someone once told me that as we think, so shall we be. At the time I was thinking of how nice it would be to have a husband who was as romantic as I am. Look at what happened."

Lou stifled a giggle so as not to hurt the older woman's feelings. "Whoever told you that lost a few marbles. You can sit in front of a tree and think about it falling on you until doomsday, and it still won't."

Standing, Celeste refilled her cup. "I see your point, but what has been, has been." Moving to a counter, she removed a canister labeled SUGAR and added two spoonfuls. "I have always had a sweet tooth, as you Americans say, as long as I can remember."

"Don't you consider yourself American?"

"Yes and no. My first allegiance has always been to France." Celeste stared out the window. "Being under United States rule has taken some getting used to, but I would rather be subject to America's flag than England's." She rose on the tips of her toes, her nose pressed to the glass pane. "How odd."

"What is?"

"There is a light in the stable. No one should be there at this hour. Maybe one of the workers left it on." Celeste opened the door. "Wait here. I must check. Last year one of our neighbors lost his barn when a horse kicked over an unattended lantern."

Lou rose and made for the other doorway. "Hold up a minute. I'll fetch one of my pistols."

"Whatever for?"

The question stopped Lou in her tracks. Why *was* she running off to get a flintlock? It wasn't as if they were in the Rockies, where hostiles, grizzlies, and painters were a constant peril.

"In all the years I've lived here, I've never been attacked.

106

Unless you count mosquitoes." Celeste laughed. "Come along if you want. We'll be perfectly safe."

"Don't mind if I do," Lou said. It was the first time she had been outside since returning from the city with her personal effects. She drank in the fresh air much as a parched wayfarer who had just crossed a desert would drink cold water. She didn't like being cooped up indoors. She never had.

"You must grow accustomed to city life again," Celeste commented, "especially now that you won't be going back into the wilderness."

Louisa thought she must have heard incorrectly. "Who says I won't?"

"I believe it was Ethel. Or was it Gladys?" Celeste tapped her chin with a painted fingernail. "I honestly can't remember. But one of them mentioned you would be staying. Your fiancé's love must be deep, indeed, for him to forsake the wilds he speaks so fondly of."

Neither of them, Lou mused, would ever give up their dream of living in the high country. The rumor perplexed her. Certainly Zach had never made any such claim. Nor had she. Where, then, had her cousins gotten the ridiculous notion? She would quiz them first thing in the morning.

The stable doors were closed but light was visible around the edges. Celeste gripped a door and started to pull, so Lou stepped forward to help. A combination of scents tingled her nose—that of recently baled hay, of musty straw piled high in a loft, of horse manure, and urine. Most stalls on either side of the wide center aisle were occupied, and several of the horses nickered as Celeste and Lou entered.

"How careless," Celeste commented, pointing at a lantern on top of the foremost stall on the left. "Who could have done such a thing?"

Lou shrugged. "Whoever it was, no harm was done."

"It was unforgivably careless," Celeste said. Walking over, she lifted the lantern off. "My father will hear of this. Whoever is to blame will be punished most severely."

A splendid white gelding was gazing at them from the opposite stall. Lou took a step, intending to pet it, then halted when loud breathing sounded behind her. Spinning, she instinctively clutched at her waist for the pistols that weren't there.

A huge brindle dog, one of half a dozen the Goujons owned, was in the doorway, its tongue lolling, its eyes glittering like coals. Almost three feet high at the shoulders, it had a enormous head, square muzzle, deep chest, and muscular legs. Lou reckoned it must weigh more than she did by a good thirty or forty pounds.

Beside the dog, holding its thick studded collar, was Racine. The Cajun bowed his head. "My apologies, Mademoiselle Clark, if I have startled you."

"Racine!" Celeste exclaimed, coming over. "What are you doing up and about at this hour? I thought you had retired hours ago."

"I did, Mademoiselle Goujon, but I could not sleep."

"A common affliction tonight," Celeste joked, smiling. Her smile died as she held up the lantern. "Someone left this burning. Have you any idea whom?"

"I'm afraid it was I." Racine jerked on the dog's collar when it tried to move toward Lou. "Behave, Louis," he said sternly.

"You?" Celeste said.

"*Oui,* mademoiselle. I looked out my window a while ago and saw Louis was loose, so I came down to catch him and put him in his pen. The stable door was open. I thought he might be in here and came in. I set the lantern down for a moment, then spied Louis outside. I ran after him without it."

"Ah. Well, as Louisa has said, no harm was done."

Lou thought it curious that Celeste was all too willing to punish any of the other servants, but Racine got off without so much as a slap on the wrist.

"I was just now returning to get it," Racine mentioned.

"We will walk with you to the pens," Celeste said, exiting. As she passed Louis the dog whined like a puppy and licked her fingers.

"There is no need. I can manage by myself."

"Of course you can." Celeste grinned. "But what man in his right mind would refuse the charming company of two lovely ladies?"

"Touché," Racine said, with another of his courtly bows. "Very well. Come, Louis." He tugged on the collar and the big dog fell into step.

"What kind is he?" Lou asked, staying well shy of the animal.

Celeste answered. "Louis is a mastiff. A very noble, very old breed. Their name comes from the Latin *massivius* which means massive. The ancient Assyrians used them to hunt lions."

"I can believe it," Lou said.

"At one time mastiffs were put in arenas to fight bears and bulls," Celeste related. "Such inhumane treatment of such gentle beasts." She bent toward Louis, who eagerly slobbered over her face and neck. Laughing, she rubbed under his chin and behind his floppy ears. "Aren't they adorable?"

Lou thought it was just about the ugliest brute she'd ever beheld. "I like smaller dogs, myself. My ma bought me a little mongrel when I was a girl. Fritz, I called him. We went everywhere together until one day he was run over by a fruit wagon. I cried and cried."

"It is tragic losing a favorite pet," Celeste agreed, patting Louis. "*Mon pere* bought the mastiffs mainly to be watch-dogs. He lets them roam the estate during the day but at night we keep them close to the mansion." She lowered her voice as if afraid others might be listening. "Some of our slaves hail from countries where dog meat is a delicacy."

"Have your mastiffs ever attacked anyone?" Lou inquired. A dog that size would be a fearsome adversary.

"Only once." This from Racine. "We had reason to believe a poacher was trapping game on the estate. Monsieur

109

Goujon sent me out with a tracker and the dogs. We found the man camped in a clearing at the edge of the great swamp. I asked him to give up peacefully but he refused, so I sicced the mastiffs on him."

"Did they kill him?" Lou asked.

"It was not a pleasant sight, mademoiselle," Racine tactfully replied.

"Don't let him scare you, Louisa," Celeste said gaily. "Out dogs are trained not to go after anyone unless given a command to do so. My father could not afford to have them decimate our slaves, now could he?"

"No, I suppose he couldn't." The remark made Lou wonder which the Goujons valued more, their dogs or the poor people who toiled in their fields.

The pen sat off by itself under a spreading elm. Each dog was housed in separate but adjoining runs. The wire-mesh door to the last one on the far right hung open. Racine guided Louis in and swiveled a short metal bar into a slot. "There. Our wandering canine friend is safe and secure."

"How did he get out in the first place?" Celeste asked.

"Louis is a smart devil," Racine said. "I've seen him pry at the bar with his paw now and then. I suspect he has figured out how to open it."

"What if he does so again tonight? He might stray off into the swamp. Or be caught and eaten."

"Before I turn in, I will tie the bar in place with rope," Racine said. "That will hold him until morning. Then I will speak to Claude about installing a lock."

Overhead, stars sparkled like fireflies. Celeste, inhaling the magnolia scented air, said dreamily, "I love summer nights. Don't you, Louisa?"

"Yes." But what Lou loved more was Zach, and she still wanted to see him before she went back to bed. "Do either of you know which room my fiancé is in?"

"*Non*, I'm afraid I do not," Celeste responded. "Jules would know but he is sound asleep, I expect. Racine, how about you?"

The Cajun seemed to hesitate. "I have no idea, mademoiselle. I recall your father instructing Jules to escort Monsieur King upstairs, but I did not hear which room. Trying to find him would be impossible at this hour. There are fifteen bedrooms on the second floor alone."

It was beyond Lou why anyone wanted or needed that many. Even more were on the third floor. "You must have a lot of big family get-togethers," she remarked.

Celeste looked at her. "Seven or eight times a year we hold gala affairs, and our guests are always welcome to stay over. Believe it or not, sometimes we do not have enough bedrooms for everyone."

They were midway to the mansion. Lou's robe was loosening so she tightened the belt. An instant later, out of the night issued a distinct thump. "Did you hear that?"

"Hear what?" Celeste said.

The thump was repeated. It came from a cluster of lilac bushes near the rear of the stable. "That," Lou said. "We should have a look-see."

Racine sprang in front of them, his arms outspread. "Permit me, ladies. There is no telling what it is. Perhaps a wild beast. Both of you should go inside while I check."

"I'll go with you," Lou said. He needed someone to watch his back.

"You have no weapon, Mademoiselle Clark."

"Neither do you."

"True. But with all due respect, I am somewhat more capable of defending myself than you. I am, after all, a master at la savate."

Celeste grasped Lou's wrist. "He has a point, *mon petit*. We will wait for him in the kitchen." To the Cajun she said, "If you are not back in five minutes, I will rouse the servants and have them search for you."

Racine faded into the darkness. Within moments he was in among the lilacs and out of sight.

"Come," Celeste said.

Although running away went against Lou's grain, she let

the older woman virtually pull her inside. Only after the door was shut did Celeste relax. Lou leaned against the counter, seeing her hostess in a whole new light. Celeste Goujon was undeniably beautiful and supremely cultured, but she lacked a few inches of raw backbone.

"I pray it is not the skunk ape again," Celeste commented, her nose pressed to the window.

"The what?"

"A creature that lives deep in the swamp. Several years ago something killed several of our cattle and two of our horses, all in one night. They were ripped apart, torn to pieces in a frenzy of bloodlust. Tracks were found, ungodly prints with only three toes and a long, narrow heel." Celeste bit her lower lip. "A nauseating stench hung around for days. The older Cajuns crossed themselves and said it was the skunk ape."

Lou had never heard of any such animal, although her prospective father-in-law once recounted a horrifying tale about his run-in with large, hairy manlike creatures high in the Rockies. Those man-beasts sounded similar to the skunk ape, only they had five toes, not three.

"It was right after the skunk ape paid us a visit that *mon pere* bought the mastiffs," Celeste said, turning. "Since then, the abomination has not bothered us. But we hear from time to time of hunters and trappers who spot it."

"And you claimed it was perfectly safe to go outside a while ago?"

A noise at the door caused them both to jump. Racine entered, grinning at their nervousness. "I looked and looked but saw nothing," he reported. "It could have been a deer, a wild boar, anything."

"I have had enough excitement for one night," Celeste declared, moving toward the hall. "How about you, Louisa? Our beds beckon, *non?*"

Lou would rather hunt for Zach. But it was dreadfully late, and it would be rude to wake up Jules to ask which room her sweetheart was in. Sighing, she said good night to the Cajun and ambled off to catch some sleep, pining to herself, *Zach, Zach, where are you? I miss you, my love.*

Approximately ten minutes before Celeste Goujon noticed a light on in the stable, the object of Louisa's affection whirled to confront a giant snarling dog. Zach's right hand fell to the one of his pistols but he didn't draw, he didn't shoot. The dog belonged to the Goujons, and he would rather not kill it if possible. They wouldn't take kindly to having one of their pets slain. Nor would they think highly of him traipsing around in the dead of night.

So, forcing a smile, Zach said softly. "Nice dog. Good dog. You remember me, don't you? I walked by the pens earlier."

Apparently the dog didn't because it coiled to spring, the short hairs at the nape of its neck bristling.

Zach had tried. He began to ease the pistol out, his thumb on the hammer.

The next second the left-hand stable door swung outward. Racine stepped out, his surprise self-evident. Regaining his composure, he addressed the huge dog. "Sit, Louis. Sit." The brute obeyed, whining.

"I'm obliged," Zach thanked him.

"Monsieur King, this is quite unexpected," the Cajun said, "and fortuitous, if I do say so, myself." He moved aside. "Come in, if you please. I was checking on a mare about to foal."

Zach remembered the woman's voice he'd heard and realized he might be making a prime jackass of himself. It was probably Gladys—she and Racine had set up a late night tryst, and he had come along and spoiled it. "I don't want to intrude," he said, backing away.

"You are not," Racine assured him. "Trust me. Join us. There is someone here who would like a few words with you."

"Oh?" Zach went in. To one side a woman waited, her features shrouded in shadow. "Gladys? Is that you?"

"No, it is not." Into the lantern light stepped Martha Clark, fully dressed, a shawl over her shoulders and head.

"Aunt Martha? What are you doing up so late?"

"Racine and I were discussing how best to scratch each other's backs. And here you waltz in and give yourself to us on a silver platter, as it were. I can't thank you enough for making it so easy."

"Ma'am?" Zach had no clue what she was talking about.

Aunt Martha smiled. But it wasn't a warm, friendly smile. It was starkly sinister, her expression fraught with hatred. "Did you honestly think, you miserable half-breed, that I'd allow my precious niece to marry scum like you?"

Dumbfounded, Zach was a shade slow in reacting to the scrape of soles behind him. He spun, but Racine was already close enough to strike, a horseshoe clenched on high. Zach tried to dodge while simultaneously sweeping an arm up to deflect the blow. He was unsuccessful. The horseshoe smashed into his temple, staggering him.

"Again!" Aunt Martha cried.

Zach clawed in vain at his weapons. His arms had lost their strength, his knees were buckling. Another jarring impact, above his right ear, pitched him to the ground. He tasted dirt, tasted blood, but attempted to rise. He couldn't. Everything was spinning around and around; the stalls, the walls, the two ominous forms that loomed above him.

"I thought for sure you had busted his skull wide open," Aunt Martha said. "His head must be harder than an anvil. Finish him off."

Gritting his teeth, Zach sought to rise. But his limbs were so much mush. He could barely think, thanks to the vicious hammering in his head. Dimly, he heard the Cajun answer her.

"I will finish him in my own way, Madame Livingston. I have it all worked out so that no suspicion will fall on either of us."

A hand gripped Zach's buckskin shirt, and he was

roughly rolled over. Aunt Martha's leering visage wavered before him.

"Can you hear me, 'breed? I want you to know this was all my doing. I have a deal with Mr. Racine, you see. I've agreed to help him press his suit with Gladys in exchange for his help in eliminating you."

Zach was fast losing consciousness. Resistance was futile. An inky veil claimed him, and how long he was out, he couldn't say. He revived to find his arms and legs bound and a gag in his mouth. Vegetation hemmed him in, smelling of lilacs. He tried to rise but his legs wouldn't support his weight. Twice more he tried but fell back down. Suddenly a darkling shape hove over him.

"*Mon Dieu.* What does it take to keep you down?"

The voice, Zach thought, was Racine's. Another blow to the temple spiked agony through his whole body and plunged him into a bottomless black pit. He felt as if he were falling—then he felt nothing at all.

Chapter Nine

The first inkling Louisa May Clark had that something was frightfully wrong occurred at breakfast. The Goujon family—father, daughter, and son—ate their morning meal punctually at seven A.M. Shortly after six Jules knocked on each guest's door to politely remind them. Lou washed in a small basin on the dresser, slipped into the new dress Aunt Martha had purchased for her the day before, and danced down the stairs in the highest of spirits.

Lou was finally going to see Zach again. She greeted Aunt Martha and Uncle Earnest cheerily, spoke with Harry a short while about various sights to visit in St. Louis, and had just taken her seat at the long table when Uncle Thomas, Ethel, and Gladys arrived. Not a minute later so did the Goujons.

Maids brought in the fare: steaming eggs piled high on solid silver trays; enough bacon and ham and sausage to

116

feed an army; toast, buns, and butter; and plenty of aromatic black coffee.

Lou stared at the doorway, anxiously awaiting her beloved. She fidgeted like a schoolgirl, so eager to embrace him she couldn't sit still. She didn't think much of it when Jules came in, walked over to Jacques and whispered into Goujon's ear. She figured it must have something to do with Jules's many domestic duties.

The maids were soon done, and Jacques rose. "My dear friends," he said suavely. "Before we begin, we must give thanks. Later, for those of you who are willing, we have another jaunt into the city planned." He folded his hands together.

"Wait," Lou said. "Zach isn't here yet. We shouldn't begin without him."

"Evidently, mademoiselle, he has no interest in eating. He was not in his room when Jules went to get him."

Louisa knew the Kings were early risers, invariably at the crack of the dawn. They didn't believe in letting a single minute of daylight go to waste. Country folk all shared that ethic, unlike their city counterparts who would rather lay about than get up and about. So it was possible, Lou mused, that Zach had gotten up at first light and gone for a stroll around the grounds. She said as much to their host.

"In that case he should show up momentarily," Jacques said. "In the meantime, we can't let the food grow cold. With your permission?"

"Sure. Go ahead." Lou bowed her head as grace was given but she didn't hear a word Jacques said. She kept peering at the doorway, hoping to see Zach. The rest started helping themselves to whatever struck their fancy, chattering like chipmunks. Lou ignored them, riveted to the doorway, a few spoonfuls of scrambled eggs all she selected.

"—dear, are you listening?"

Lou became aware Aunt Martha was addressing her. "I'm sorry. I didn't hear what you said," she replied.

"That much was obvious." Aunt Martha was buttering a

piece of toast. "What has you so distracted? Your fiancé? He'll show up soon. Quit worrying." She took a bite. "He wouldn't have gone off anywhere without telling you."

"No, he wouldn't," Lou agreed. She nibbled at her eggs, forking tiny bits into her mouth. The minutes dragging by weighted with millstones.

"I was thinking, dear," Aunt Martha said, "of buying you additional clothes today. A woman should have more than one decent dress to her name."

"Whatever you want," Lou absently responded.

"Good. Maybe we'll buy you a hat, too. One of those chic feathered headpieces all the young ladies are wearing."

Lou despised hats. On hot days they made her scalp itch and on cold, blustery days, the wind always threatened to rip them off her head. "No hat," she said, a tad gruffly.

"Whatever you want. But it won't hurt to try a few on, will it? Just to see if any complement you and your new outfits."

Lou glanced at the empty chair on her right, its emptiness symbolic of the emptiness in her heart. She missed Zach more and more with each passing second. It was probably silly, but an overwhelming urge to see him had gripped her, an urge that would not be denied. Setting down her fork and placing her cloth napkin beside her plate, she rose. "If all of you will excuse me, I'm going to find Zach."

"In the middle of the meal?" Uncle Earnest said, frowning in disapproval. "Surely it can wait."

"No, it can't."

"Want me to come along?" Harry asked.

"That's all right." Lou would rather be alone when she found him. She hurried on around the head of the table, mechanically smiling at Jacques and Auguste.

The elder Goujon swiveled in his chair toward Jules, who stood as straight as a broomstick nearby. "Accompany Mademoiselle Clark upstairs. Show her where Monsieur King's room is."

"Oui, Monsieur." Jules bowed. "If you will follow me, Mademoiselle Clark."

Lou impatiently did just that, climbing all the way to the third floor and going down the hall to the last room on the left. "Are any of these other rooms occupied?" she inquired as they came to a halt.

"Several of the servants, myself and Racine included, have rooms at the other end. But Monsieur King has this half of the floor all to himself."

It incensed Lou that Zach had been segregated, as if he were somehow unworthy of having a room next to anyone else. "Why didn't you put him on the second floor with my relatives?"

"You sound upset, mademoiselle. But I only did as Racine instructed me. He mentioned that Monsieur King would have more privacy this way." Jules knocked twice and waited for a response.

"Try again," Lou prompted.

Jules did so, louder, but again silence mocked them. He tried the latch. "It is unlocked. Should we go in? I am not allowed to enter a guest's room without permission."

"Open it." Lou shouldered past him as he did. Immediately, she saw that a mistake had been made. The bed hadn't been slept in. The green quilt and fluffy pillows were undisturbed. None of Zach's personal effects were in evidence, either. Lou yanked open the closet, hoping to see his rifle and parfleches, but the closet was empty. "You must have the wrong room."

"Non, mademoiselle. This is the one I brought your fiancé to. I am positive."

"Then where are all his things? Where is *he?"* Convinced Jules had blundered, Lou went back out and tried the next door. The room was likewise empty, the bed made up. Growing more and more disturbed, Lou checked each and every room between the end of the hall and the stairs. The result was the same.

"This can't be," Lou said, resisting an inner flood tide of dismay. "This simply can't be."

Jules was genuinely concerned. "I share your worry. But perhaps there is a simple explanation both of us have overlooked."

"Such as?"

"Perhaps Monsieur Clark requested a new room. If he did not like being by himself, it is entirely possible he asked to be moved to the second floor with the rest of the men. Racine would know, if anyone would."

Without wasting a second, Lou wheeled and hastened down to the dining room. Everyone else was still there, most done their meal but lingering over aromatic coffee or tea. She marched straight to the head of the table.

"Get that manservant of yours in here. I want to know where the blazes my fiancé is."

Jacques Goujon was raising a cup to his mouth. "Pardon?"

"Zach isn't in the room Jules put him in, and all his stuff is gone. So he must have switched to another one. Racine should know, right?"

"We will get to the bottom of this right away," Jacques said. "Jules, find Racine and bring him here this instant. We must clear up this mystery. I do not like having my guests unduly upset." He smiled at Lou as Jules rushed off to do his bidding. "Please, do not worry. We will find Monsieur King. Why not enjoy a glass of fruit juice while we wait?"

Lou wasn't budging until Zach arrived. Tapping her foot in annoyance, she responded, "If it's all the same to you, I'll stay right here."

Celeste had been listening to their exchange. "I hope Monsieur King is not off in the woods somewhere. Not after that sound we heard last night."

"Sound?" her father said.

Lou paced as Celeste detailed their minor adventure with the mastiff the night before. Her sole interest was on the doorway. A gnawing core of anxiety grew deep within her, a sense that there was more to her beloved's absence than merely changing rooms. She tingled with unease when Jules materialized, Racine in tow.

The tall Cajun glanced at Gladys and received a warm smile.

Jacques got right to the point. "Where is Monsieur King, Racine? He is not in the room Jules assigned him, nor has he showed up for breakfast."

Racine avoided Lou's penetrating gaze. Hands clasped behind his back, feet wide, he resembled a soldier at attention. "I regret to inform you, monsieur, and Mademoiselle Clark, that her fiancé departed the plantation at dawn."

Lou was incredulous.

"Departed?" Jacques said. "Where on earth to?"

"It was my understanding he was going back to the mountains, to the Rockies," Racine said. "I happened to run into him in the hall. He had his long rifle and his peculiar buckskin bags with him."

Jacques and Auguste both rose, the father saying, "And he told you in so many words that he was leaving for the Rockies?"

"*Oui,*" Racine answered. "He told me he was fed up with civilization. That he wanted to go back to the mountains where he belonged."

Everyone in the dining room had stopped talking.

"But what about Mademoiselle Clark?" Auguste said. "Did Monsieur King mention her at all?"

Racine looked down at the floor. "*Oui.* He said it was best for them both if he left. He said she would be happier in Ohio with her family than up in the mountains with him. He was very sad when he said it, almost in tears."

"Oh, my," Celeste said.

Lou's head was spinning. For a few seconds she feared Zach had truly gone, that it was some sort of noble sacrifice on his part. Hadn't she gushed on and on about how happy she was to be with her kin again? Maybe he had taken it the wrong way. Then common sense took over. Memories of their many loving moments flashed through her mind, remembrances of their many tender embraces, their pledges of unending devotion. Her whole body grew hot with anger and she stalked up to Racine. "You're a liar."

The Cajun's head jerked up. "Mademoiselle?"

"You heard me," Lou said, clenching her fists. "You're a lying son of a bitch."

Celeste Goujon gasped. Most everyone else was too shocked to do or say anything. After fifteen seconds of absolute quiet, Jacques, wearing a kindly look, put his hand on Lou's shoulder. "Now, now, mademoiselle—"

Lou shrugged the hand off, then poked Racine in the chest. "I don't know why you're doing this, but you'd better tell me where Zach is, right this instant, or there will be hell to pay."

Aunt Martha pushed to her feet. "Now see here, young lady. That's quite enough out of you. Don't hold Mr. Racine to account for what your fiancé has done."

"You're siding with him?" Lou asked, hurt that her aunt could do such a thing.

"What reason would he have to lie?" Aunt Martha said, coming toward them. "Now that I think about it, your Zachary didn't seem to be entirely comfortable here. Why that was, I can't say. Lord knows, we went out of our way to make him feel welcome."

"That we did," Uncle Earnest echoed.

"I said I was sorry for how I'd behaved," Uncle Thomas threw in. "I hope he didn't leave on account of me."

"He didn't leave period," Lou declared. She was unable to fathom how they so readily accepted Racine's explanation.

"But he *is* gone," Aunt Martha said. "He even took his belongings with him. What more proof do you need?" She paused. "I don't want you to misconstrue what I'm about to say. But perhaps, just perhaps, mind you, it might work out for the best. If your fiancé would up and leave you without saying good-bye, he can't love you as much as you thought he did."

Lou grew hotter, her nails biting into her palms, her knuckles white. "I'll say this one last time. Zach would never, ever desert me." She faced Racine again. "Last chance. Where is he?"

"I honestly do not know, mademoiselle."

Lou had had enough. She pushed him aside, fury propelling her, her dress swishing with every stride.

"Louisa!" Aunt Martha called. "Where are you going?"

"To find the man I love." Lou felt tears creeping into her eyes, but she blinked them away. Now wasn't the time to be emotional. She needed a clear head. Her best recourse, she decided, was to scour the grounds and ask every servant and slave she saw whether they had seen Zach.

Lou headed for the kitchen, intending to take a shortcut through it. The feel of the dress on her legs brought her to a halt. She glanced down at it, at Aunt Martha's gift. Suddenly she loathed it. She never had been fond of dresses, preferring boy's clothes to the dainty frills women wore. But the one she now had on seemed doubly loathsome. Rotating on a heel, she flew upstairs to her room.

When Lou emerged some ten minutes later she wore buckskins fashioned for her by Winona King, Zach's mother. Strapped around her slender waist were two pistols and a Green River knife. Across her chest were slanted an ammunition pouch, powder horn, and possibles bag. Cradled in her left arm was the Hawken given to her by Nate King, Zach's father.

Her eyes as steely as the fire steel she carried in the possibles bag, Lou went back down. She had to pass the dining room to reach the kitchen. Her relatives, who were just filing out, gawked at her as if she were a spectral apparition.

"What in the world?" Aunt Martha exclaimed. "Where did you get those awful clothes and all those weapons?"

Lou recalled that her aunt and the others had never seen

123

her in her frontier garb. "They're mine," she said brusquely, about to walk on by. Uncle Earnest deliberately stepped in front of her, blocking her way.

"Really, Lou. I think this nonsense has gone far enough. There's no need for this childish display of pique."

Lou swung the Hawken around so the muzzle was pointed at her uncle's left foot. "Ever seen a man's toes blown off?"

Earnest's mouth fell open. Gladys covered hers with a hand. Ethel, astounded, bleated, "Goodness gracious. She's gone savage on us."

Aunt Martha put her hands on her stout hips. "Don't take out your frustrations on us, little one. We're your own flesh and blood, remember? No one cares more for you or cares more about your welfare than we do."

"Prove it," Lou said. "Help me find Zach."

Harry was the only one who stepped forward. "I'll lend you a hand, Louisa," he volunteered. "What do you want me to do?"

Lou smiled at him. Of all of them, Simpleton Harry, as his father used to call him, was the only one willing to stand by her. It moved her mightily.

Uncle Earnest wagged a finger at his son. "You'll do no such thing. Her antics are atrocious, and until she comes to her senses and apologizes for her unseemly conduct we won't lift a finger to help."

"That's not right," Harry said.

"You let me decide what's right and what isn't," Earnest declared in a condescending manner. "As of right now, little Miss Savage is on her own."

The barb cut Louisa to the quick but she refused to give them the satisfaction of knowing it. She barreled past Earnest. No one else tried to stop her, which was just as well. In her mood she was liable to hurt them.

The Goujons's cook, or chef, as they referred to him, along with a kitchen staff of four, was busy cleaning up. They all wore crisp white uniforms. In addition, the bearded chef wore a high conical white hat that resembled a watermelon set on end. How he could work and keep the thing on his head, Lou would never know. They gaped at her, at the intruder in their domain, but not one demanded to know what she was doing there. One look at the Hawken, the pistols, and her expression was enough to warn them that discretion was the better part of curiosity.

Lou stopped and nodded at the chef. "I'm looking for Zachary King, my fiancé. Have you seen him?"

The man's bushy brows pinched together in befuddlement. *"Tres bien, merci. Te vous?"*

"Do you speak English?" Lou asked.

"Anglais? Non. Je parle Francais. Comprenez-vous?"

Huffing in exasperation, Lou went on out. The morning sun was so bright she had to squint against the glare. Ten yards from the mansion it hit her that she didn't really know where to begin. She needed to think, to work out how to proceed. Glancing back, she saw the faces of some of the kitchen workers at the window. Others were watching from the second floor—Aunt Martha and Uncle Earnest. Both were scowling.

The open stable doors beckoned. As Lou crossed the yard a noise from the direction of the dog pens snapped her head around. A man was working on the door to Louis's run, probably installing the new lock.

Inside the stable it was shaded and cool. Lou leaned against the wall, her shoulders slumped. She refused to give in to despair. She must access the situation anew, sort through the facts. First and foremost, Zach would never leave her. Never, ever. Since that was patently true, it completely baffled her why Racine would claim otherwise. What possible purpose did his lie serve?

Lou bit her lip. She would consider his motive later. For now, finding Zach was all that counted. Where to begin? she asked herself. The last time she saw him had been about ten o'clock. Between then and seven he'd vanished, a nine-hour span. Anything could have happened in that amount of time.

Stop it! Lou railed at herself. She had to stop thinking the worst. Zach was still alive. She was sure of it. Although she couldn't say exactly how she knew, she felt deep down inside that he was. But he might be in great danger, so she must find him swiftly.

Where to begin? Racine claimed that Zach had left at dawn, about three hours ago. Left how? Lou wondered. On foot? No, Zach wouldn't bother to hike all the way into St. Louis. If he had a horse, he would ride, but since he didn't, that left the same means of transportation the Goujons and their guests always used.

A scraping sound alerted Lou that she wasn't alone. She straightened, the Hawken rising level at her waist.

An elderly black man in drab homespun clothes was sweeping the central aisle. His back was to her and he hadn't noticed her yet.

"Good morning," Lou said.

The man slowly turned. He had a full beard, full cheeks, and large eyes that widened even more. "Land o' goshen! You ain't fixin' to shoot ol' Jess, are you, gal?"

Lou cradled the Hawken. "Why would I want to do a silly thing like that?" She gestured at the interior of the stable. "This where you work?"

"Yes, ma'am," Jess said. "Going on nigh forty years now. I keep the stable clean and take care of the horses." He gazed fondly down the aisle. "It's good work. Better than being out in the fields, I can tell you. Monsieur Goujon did me a great kindness the day he picked me to be his stableman."

"Do you help get the carriage ready when it leaves?" Lou casually inquired.

"Yes, ma'am. I usually lead the whites out. They can be skittish around folks they don't know. They even act up on Willis, the driver, sometimes." Jess stepped to the first stall on the right and a white gelding nuzzled his outstretched

126

hand. "Isn't he something? They're like my children to me. I love them all dearly."

"Are they tired from that ride into the city this morning?"

"Ma'am?"

"I thought I heard someone mention at breakfast that the carriage had gone into St. Louis earlier."

"Oh, no, ma'am. My children haven't been out all morning. I just got through givin' each of them a rubdown."

"Thank you, Jess." Lou strode back out, toward the mansion. Now she had proof Racine was lying through his teeth. He would own up to it or suffer the consequences. But halfway there she slowed, her fury dissipating. Her worry over Zach was leading her astray. Racine would never admit to his lie. He'd concoct another, maybe that Zach had in fact left on foot.

Aunt Martha, still at the second floor window, smiled and waved.

Lou didn't return the gesture. Reversing direction, she took to the path that linked the grounds to the fields. She did so more to escape her aunt's spying than anything else. Presently the high grass on either side gave way to cultivated crops. Soybeans, corn, and other vegetables were prominent. Slaves toiled among the rows, some singing as they worked, musical chants in a foreign tongue.

Lou couldn't see what they had to sing about. Many had been dragged from their homelands, thrown into the filthy holds of slaver ships, and been borne clear across the ocean to labor the rest of their days away in squalid poverty, subject to the whims of their self-appointed lords and masters.

A rider came into view, a short man on a sorrel. A broadbrimmed brown hat crowned his sweaty face, which was dotted with stubble. His clothes were sweat-stained, his black boots badly scuffed. In his right hand was a whip. Not a riding whip, but a long bullwhip, the type that could take a person's ear off at twenty feet. He drew rein, his thick lips creased in an amused smirk.

"How-do, missy." The man touched the bullwhip to his

hat brim. "Might I ask who you are? And what you're doing out here?"

"I'm one of Monsieur Goujon's guests," Lou responded
stiffly. "If it's any of your business."

"No disrespect meant," the man said. "I'm Harold Edgerton, the overseer. It isn't often any of the guests stray
this far from the mansion."

"I needed to get out and stretch my legs," Lou lied. She
didn't like the man, didn't like how his beady eyes roved
up and down her body.

"Dressed like that? I've never seen a woman in buckskins before. Hell, I've never seen a woman in britches. It
takes some getting used to." Edgerton hooked a leg over
the saddle. "All those guns, I figured maybe you were out
hunting."

Lou had an inspiration. "My fiancé came out to hunt
earlier, about daybreak. Maybe you've run into him? His
name is Zach King."

Edgerton shook his head. "You're the only person other
than the slaves I've seen all day, and I was out in the fields
before the roosters crowed." The overseer pushed his hat
back on his head. "No. Wait. Come to think of it, I did see
Mateo."

"Who?"

"A Cajun, missy. He does a lot of tracking and hunting
for Monsieur Goujon. Spends most of his time in the woods
or off in the swampland."

"And he was alone?"

"Sure was. Had his pack horse with him. But instead of
the usual supplies, it was carrying a big bundle wrapped in
a canvas. He told me he was on an errand for his friend, a
fellow you've likely met. Racine, Monsieur Goujon's manservant."

Lou's heart quaked. *A big bundle wrapped in a canvas?*
Her mouth went dry and she had to wet it before she could
ask, "Did Mateo happen to say exactly what was in the
canvas?"

"No, he sure didn't. But you can find out for yourself." Harold Edgerton pointed with the bullwhip, toward the mansion.

Stalking in their direction was Racine.

Chapter Ten

Zachary King clutched at fleeting sensations as a drowning man would clutch at floating logs. He seemed to be rising up out of a deep, dark well, slowly clawing toward a pinprick of light far, far overhead. Gradually feeling seeped through him. He was aware of the hot sun on his face, of being in motion. His wrists and ankles ached abominably from rope tied tight. His head, though, hurt much worse; incessant, excruciating pounding rendered it difficult for him to think.

Zach's mouth was bone-dry, his throat parched. He sorely craved water. So when he heard a light splash he thought it must be his imagination, but then he heard it again and again, rhythmic stroking such as a paddle might make. Someone coughed.

Zach had the presence of mind not to sit up or otherwise do anything that would let whoever was close by know he was awake. Cracking an eyelid, he discovered he was in the bow of a canoe.

In the stern, on his knees, hunched a stocky man with black curly hair. He bore the stamp of a woodsman in his bronzed, weathered features. His broad shoulders and powerful arms levered the paddle with skilled efficiency. Two pistols adorned his waist, along with a bone-handled knife. In front of him lay a doubled-edged ax.

Zach's eyes flicked right and left. Lush vegetation formed near solid walls. Willow trees and others he couldn't identify reared on high, laden with clinging vines and thick with leaves. The air was pregnant with heat, as well as the musk of dank earth and rank water.

Their canoe was winding along a ribbon of murky water that meandered haphazardly through the growth, seldom proceeding in a straight line for more than twenty yards. Zach had never been in a swamp before but he'd enough heard about them to guess he was being taken into the depths of the swampland that bordered the Goujon plantation.

A sense that something was amiss filled him. Zach secretly scoured the vegetation, trying to pinpoint what it was. The next splash of the paddle solved the mystery. It was the *only* sound to be heard. The swamp was eerily, deathly quiet, unnaturally so, since by rights the trees should teem with birds and small game.

"It is most strange, is it not?" the stocky man said. When Zach didn't respond, he chuckled. "You can quit pretending, Monsieur King. It is not easy to trick Mateo."

Since he had been found out, Zach opened his eyes. The throbbing grew worse. Flinching, he tried to shift position to relieve a cramp in his arms, which had been tied behind his back. The cramped confines of the canoe hampered him. "What is so strange?" he asked.

Mateo's dark eyes probed the undergrowth. "The silence. I have experienced this before. Always, I have a feeling I am being watched.

Zach had a greater concern. Licking his dry lips, he asked, "Where are you taking me? What is this all about?"

"I thought you knew about Racine and Mademoiselle Clark? The pretty one, Gladys? He is quite taken with her."

Dimly, Zach recollected Aunt Martha telling him she had agreed to help Racine win favor with Gladys in exchange for Racine's help in disposing of him. "You intend to kill me."

"I would, if that were what Racine asked me to do. He and I have been good friends since we were no bigger than bullfrogs." Mateo grinned, showing a gap where two of his upper front teeth had been. "I have never had trouble killing. Man or beast, it makes no difference. But Racine is more softhearted. He could not bring himself to slay you outright. No, he came up with a more ingenuous way."

Zach tried to move his hands but his wrists were expertly bound. "You're going to feed me to alligators?"

Mateo showed he had a third missing tooth. "You are thinking of New Oreleans, monsieur. Some of the old-timers say that many years ago gators were found this far north. But I have never seen one in my lifetime. And I know this swamp better than most."

The canoe glided out from under the canopy of trees into brighter sunlight. Water stretched for as far as the eye could see, broken by islands of vegetation and scattered hummocks. As if on signal, insects commenced buzzing. Birds trilled and chirped in avian chorus.

Mateo worked the paddle flawlessly. "The old men, they also say this swamp was once twice the size it is now. It has shrunk over the years. Maybe because the river channel has shifted. Or because there have been fewer floods." He avoided the jagged stump of a tree that had broken off at water level. "Who knows. Another fifty years and this swamp might not be here."

Zach couldn't care less. "If there aren't any alligators, how do you intend to do it?"

"We will let nature take its course." Bending forward,

Mateo applied more strength to each stroke. The canoe shot forward. "It is Racine's idea. This way, if by some miracle your body is ever found, they will blame it on your own stupidity in wandering off into the wilds."

"My fiancée will never believe I did any such thing."

"No? It doesn't matter. She will never find you, not out here. We are many miles from the estate."

Zach squinted at the sun. It was well past noon.

Mateo deduced what he was thinking. "We left shortly before dawn, so we have been on the go for over six hours. I would estimate we have gone fifteen miles." A sinuous shape cleaved the nearby water and Mateo bobbed his head at it. "Fifteen miles of cottonmouths and copperheads. Fifteen miles of massasaugas and snapping turtles. Of mosquitoes, bogs, and quicksand. It is they who will kill you, Monsieur King. You will never make it out of the swamp alive."

The serpentine form dived and was gone. Zach surveyed the seemingly limitless expanse of watery morass, trying to convince himself that surviving wouldn't be the challenge Mateo made it out to be. But he had never been one to deny the truth, and the truth was that he knew next to nothing about swamps. He had been born and bred in the mountains. Here, he was as much out of his element as an Eastern dandy would be in the high country.

"You might last three or four days," Mateo said. "If you can find safe water to drink, and game to eat, and keep from being bitten by poisonous snakes."

"Or attacked by the skunk ape," Zach said.

"Ah. You have heard of it, have you?" Mateo laughed. "I have seen it, you know. Twice, at a distance. But it is not as fearsome as the oldsters claim. Each time it ran off."

"What you're doing is wrong," Zach commented. "Have you no honor?" To a Shoshone warrior honor was as important as counting coup.

"I honor my close friend, Racine, by helping him win

the heart of the woman he adores." Mateo straightened, peering intently ahead. "There it is."

"It" turned out to be a small, virtually barren islet, twenty yards from end to end and about half that wide. Except for a patch of grass at the southern tip it was covered with mottled rocks. Mateo guided the canoe toward the grassy end, using the paddle to slow their momentum. "You are probably wondering why I came so far?"

Zach assumed it was to reduce his chances of making it back alive but he didn't say so.

"Most of the islands are covered by trees and bushes but not this one," Mateo noted, slowing even more. "Maybe that is why the snakes like it so much. In the afternoon they come here to sun themselves. See for yourself, Monsieur King."

Despite himself, Zach looked again. It took a moment for what he was seeing to register. The rocks weren't mottled; the spots and blotches of color were the scaly skins of a swarm of reptiles. The islet crawled with them, some basking in the sun, others wending and weaving among one another, their tongues constantly darting out and in. His skin rippled with goose bumps.

Mateo brought the canoe in alongside the patch of grass. He poked at the stems with his paddle a number of times, then carefully checked the surrounding water before easing over the side. Placing the paddle on the bottom, he moved forward and reached in to grab Zach. "Let's get this over with, monsieur. I want to get back before the sun goes down. Even I, who am so at home here, do not like to be abroad at night."

Zach tensed his legs.

"I warn you," Mateo said. "Do not try anything or I will make this much harder than Racine wants." Gripping the front of Zach's buckskin shirt, he pulled Zach into a sitting position, then cursed when the canoe started to swing away from the islet. Letting go, he grasped the bow and hauled the canoe a foot or so onto the grassy point. The whole while Mateo kept his eyes on the grass, alert for stray serpents. From the jumbled rocks issued sibilant hissing. The snakes were agitated by the intrusion.

"The sooner I leave, the happier I will be." Mateo grabbed Zach under the arms and half raised, half dragged him over the side and into the grass.

"You intend to just leave me here?" Zach said, flexing his knees to restore circulation.

"That is the general idea, yes," Mateo said, grinning. "If you lie real still the snakes will not bother you. Later, though, when it grows cool, they will leave the rocks. Some will come through this grass. Your warm body will attract them, and they will curl up around you and under you." He paused. "How long after that, do you think, until you make the mistake of moving and one bites you?"

Zach glanced toward the rocks. So this was what the man had meant about letting nature take its course. "If my body is found anytime soon, the rope will still be on my wrists and ankles. Everyone will know I was murdered."

"What, you expect me to untie you?" Mateo laughed, then rubbed his jaw. "You have a point, though." Turning, he waded out and retrieved the ax. "A few blows from this will insure you do not go anywhere until the cottonmouths and massasaugas do what they are supposed to."

Zach wriggled backward, toward the rocks. At any moment an errant viper might rear and strike but that was the risk he had to take.

"No, you don't," Mateo said, suddenly darting around to stand between Zach and the rocks. "That's as far as you go."

Zach shifted, using his elbows to rotate his whole body. The head of the ax gleamed brightly in the sunlight as Mateo patted it. Zach had his knees bent, his thigh muscles braced, but he needed to lure the man nearer. "To kill someone who is tied up takes a lot of courage. You're one rotten son of a bitch, you know that?"

Mateo hefted the ax higher. "I'm going to enjoy this,

boy." Lunging, he swept it in a wide arc, aiming the flat of the blade at Zach's temple.

Were the blow to land it would spell Zach's doom. He would be knocked unconscious, untied, and left for the reptiles or the elements to finish off. Zach wasn't going to let that happen. He wrenched his head to one side, and the ax thudded into the soil instead of into his skull. For an instant Mateo was above him, slightly off balance, and Zach drove his legs up and out, thrusting with all his might, his feet slamming into the cutthroat's sternum.

Tottering, Mateo flailed his arms to restore his balance. Zach flung himself into a roll, and just as Mateo straightened Zach rammed his feet into the man again, this time into Mateo's legs.

"Damn you!" Mateo staggered back again, almost to the end of the grass.

Zach threw caution aside and rolled a second time. Only now it was his shoulders he drove into Mateo's shins, throwing his entire weight into it. Mateo yipped like a kicked cur as he was bowled over and keeled backward, onto the hot rocks—and onto the snakes.

Zach saw raw terror in the man's eyes. Writhing forms were under Mateo's arms, under his legs, and all around him. The hissing rose to a frenzied crescendo. As Zach looked on, a slender shape reared, mouth agape, curved fangs distended.

Mateo still had the double-edged ax. He swung it one-handed, the razor-honed steel shearing the serpent's head clean off. Then he heaved to his feet, seeking to reach the safety of the grass, but he was barely up off the ground when another snake went to strike. With a sideways swipe, he cleaved it in two.

Other serpents scattered, some were coiled, some were fighting one another. Mateo, gripping the ax handle with both hands, swiveled so he could keep his eyes on them. He took a single step backward—then cried out when a splotched serpent flashed out of a narrow cleft and sank its dripping fangs into his calf.

Mateo automatically bent down and clutched his leg. "No!" he railed. "No, no, no!" Teetering, he took another step. He spotted a thick snake coming toward him and split its head down the center, but even as he dispatched it another reptile buried its tapered fangs in his other leg.

Howling, Mateo skipped into the grass and halted, breathing heavily, more from fear than the venom now in his bloodstream. "This can not be!" he said. "This just can not be!"

Zach was watching to see if any of the snakes entered the grass but apparently none did.

Mateo slowly pivoted. His features hardened, his voice falling to a gravely rasp. "This is all your fault. You did this to me."

"You brought it on yourself," Zach said, sliding away. He wondered how long it would take the poison to take effect and whether enough had been injected to do the job.

"I'm a dead man," Mateo said, his voice breaking. He looked down at his legs, at the blood trickling from the bites. "But I won't die alone. You hear me? It doesn't matter now if anyone finds your body."

Zach levered his legs and elbows, gaining another yard. But he was only prolonging the inevitable. The woodsman could kill him with ease.

"I will chop your arms off first," Mateo said, lurching forward. "Then your legs. And last of all, your head."

Bringing his knees up to his chest, Zach prepared to defend himself as best he could.

Mateo raised the ax to shoulder height. His face was marred by pain and his left leg began to quiver uncontrollably. "I should have drowned you. I should have tied rocks to you and let you sink to the bottom."

Zach was almost to the water. Another foot or so and he would run out of space. He placed his back flat for extra leverage.

"Die, bastard!" Mateo elevated the ax, his whole body trembling as if from a fit. Firming his grip, he clenched his teeth and brought the ax sweeping down, at Zach's left shoulder.

Zach flipped to the right. The ax bit into the earth, missing him by a cat's whisker. Driving his legs up at an angle, he smashed his heels into Mateo's knee. A loud crack elicited a yelp.

Mateo stumbled but did not go down. "Nice try, but you won't get another." He swayed, his face pasty, his skin covered with perspiration. Blinking a few times as if he were having a hard time focusing, he grunted and lifted the ax for another assault.

Zach slid back further. Suddenly his elbows grew damp, and he felt water seeping along his forearms. Mateo was almost upon him. Zach tried to kick Mateo's legs but Mateo sidestepped and arched his spine.

"Now it ends!"

The ax glittered as it swept down. But midway into the swing Mateo's strength failed him and he lurched to one side. Instead of splitting Zach open, the ax split the soil. Mateo, doubling over, leaned on the handle to keep from falling, and glared. His body began to convulse, his legs quaking violently. Swearing luridly, he sank onto one knee. His skin was now so white he resembled a ghost. After thirty seconds he lowered onto his rump, his hands sliding off the handle. "You have done made worm food of me, boy."

Zach said nothing.

Mateo feebly tried to grip the ax again but he was too weak. Grinning drunkenly, he muttered in amazement, "Who ever thought it would end like this? I always figured I'd go in my sleep in old age."

"None of us know when our time will come." Zach quoted his father. It could be the next day, the next year, or in the next ten minutes. "The important thing isn't how long we live," his pa once said. "It's *how* we live the span allotted to us. Whatever you do, son, don't waste your life. Make the most of every moment."

"Done in by a stupid kid," Mateo grumbled.

"I've counted coup on Blackfeet," Zach said, feeling silly doing so.

"Is that supposed to impress me?" Mateo gasped, gurgled, and sank onto his side. His chest still moved, his eyes were alert, but the light of intellect was fast fading. "Racine claimed this would be easy. It's the only time he has ever been wrong about anything."

"I'll tell him that right before I kill him."

Snorting, Mateo attempted to speak but the venom had complete hold and all he could do was mew pathetically. His left hand rose, fell, rose again, his fingers pointed accusingly at Zach. What he wanted to say would never be known because he closed his eyes and commenced shaking from head to toe. His breathing became labored, more so with every passing second.

Zach had other concerns now that he was out of danger. He crawled toward the ax, intending to cut the ropes and free himself, but movement in the grass stopped him cold. A snake was gliding toward him. It was brownish gray with dark brown blotches ringed by black. The belly, what Zach could see of it, was black with lighter markings. Stocky in build, it bore dark bars that extended from its eyes to the rear of its jaw.

Zach had never seen a snake like it before and couldn't say what it was, but he did know it was deadly and that was enough. He scooted backward, partly into the water, giving the snake plenty of room to slink off. Only it didn't. It slowed and raised its head, its vertical pupils fixed on him, then yawned its maw wide, exposing retractable fangs much like a rattler's.

Ordinarily, snakes wouldn't attack unless provoked. Zach hadn't done anything to provoke this one, but for all he knew it was one of those agitated when Mateo fell, and it would vent its anger on him. Twisting, he struggled to rise onto his knees. His body protested, his head hammered mercilessly, his limbs hurt almost as bad.

The splotched snake moved nearer, hissing now.

Zach girded himself. His only recourse was to dive and swim—but he couldn't with his arms and legs tied—or to clamber into the canoe. Digging the balls of his feet into the ground, he shot a last glance at Mateo, whose face was discolored blue and purple, then he shoved upward. He cleared the side of the canoe, as he'd hoped, but as he fell into it headfirst, his legs banged against the side. The jolt sent the canoe sliding into the water.

Attempting to rise, Zach set it to rocking so severely it almost flipped over. He rose up high enough to see that the snake had stopped and was just lying there, staring. Congratulating himself on his narrow escape, he gazed out over the swampland. Only then did it hit him. His congratulations were premature. He had gone from the proverbial frying pan into the fire. Here he was, alone and adrift in a canoe in the middle of nowhere, his arms and legs bound, with no weapons, no food, and no water. Unless he could free himself and find his way out, he faced the prospect of a slow, lingering, excruciating death.

It might well turn out that Mateo had been the lucky one.

Louisa May Clark faced the tall Cajun, her finger on the trigger of her Hawken. She had never considered herself a bloodthirsty person but she dearly wanted to put a slug through his heart. That she didn't was due more to the fact only Racine might know where Zach was than to her self-control. "What do you want?" she demanded when he was barely within earshot.

Racine didn't answer until he came to a halt. "Monsieur Edgerton," he said, with a curt nod to the overseer. To Lou he stated, "Monsieur Goujon directed me to come after you. I am to apologize for anything I have done that has upset you, and beg you to return to the mansion."

"No."

"Please, mademoiselle. Need I remind you that you are a guest here, and that the polite thing to do is honor your host's request?"

"And need I remind you that you are a lying son of a bitch who doesn't know what honor is?"

Racine's fingers clenched and unclenched. "If you were not a woman—"

"Don't let that stop you," Lou taunted. She would like any excuse to shoot him in the leg, say, or the shoulder. A little persuasion might loosen his lips.

The Cajun was most displeased. "It is obvious that being civil is a waste of my time. But as Monsieur Edgerton is my witness, I have tried. I can go back and inform Monsieur Goujon that you refuse to listen to reason. And I will recommend that you be brought back under guard, if need be, to keep you from wandering off and coming to harm."

Lou laughed. "I'd like to see someone try to take me back. These guns aren't for bluff or ballast, mister."

"A woman wearing firearms," Racine said in contempt. "It is highly improper, if not vulgar. Your aunt and uncle agree. They think you have spent too much time in the wilderness. You need refinement, mademoiselle. You need to live among your own kind again. To relearn how women should deport themselves."

"Funny thing," Lou said. "Back here in the States women are treated like property. They're supposed to bow and scrape to their menfolk and act all prissy. But on the frontier it's different. Men treat their women as equals. It comes from sharing the same dangers, the same hardships, side by side. The men don't boss the women around as much as menfolk do here."

Racine drew himself up to his full height. "I refuse to debate ethics with someone too young to know the meaning of the word. Frontiersmen are barbarians. They visit the city from time to time, drinking and brawling and telling their tall tales. They are as far removed from true gentlemen as a trollop is from a lady."

141

"I might be young," Lou conceded. "I might not be as worldly as you. But one thing I do know. I'll never kowtow to anyone. Not to you. Not to Mr. Goujon. Not to my Aunt Martha or either of my uncles. I have too much respect for myself."

"I pity you. You are a sorely misguided young woman."

"Pity yourself if I don't find Zach."

"Is that your final word?"

"Need you ask?" Lou rejoined.

The tall Cajun spun on a heel, saying over his broad shoulder, "Very well. Just remember, though. As we reap, so do we sow."

Lou mulled over his last puzzling comment as Racine wended off along the trail. She had nearly forgotten about the overseer, but a chuckle reminded her she wasn't alone.

"That was something, girl. It's about time someone put that pompous upstart in his place. I never have liked him much, always looking down his nose at me like he does." Edgerton hefted his bullwhip. "If I can be of any help finding your man, you only have to ask."

"Do you have any idea where Mateo went after you saw him?" Lou couldn't stop thinking about that big bundle wrapped in canvas.

"He was headed for the swampland, most likely to the dock. He goes out every other day or so." Edgerton reined his mount around. "I can show you, if you'd like."

"I'd like nothing more," Lou said. She would question Mateo, and if he gave her the same evasive answers Racine did, he'd regret it. "Let's go."

The overseer held the sorrel to a brisk walk. He chatted on about how hard his work was and how long he'd been at it, but Lou didn't listen. A mile of travel through tilled fields industriously being worked by scores of slaves brought them to the lowland adjacent to the Mississippi. Two canoes were tied to a rickety plank dock. In the shade of a willow a mare had been tethered.

"That's Mateo's pack animal," Edgerton said. "One of the canoes is gone, just like I figured."

Louisa walked onto the short dock to a narrow ladder and climbed down into one of the canoes. Casting off the tie rope took but a second. She helped herself to a paddle resting on the bottom, setting the Hawken in its place.

"Now hold on, there," the overseer said, dismounting. "It isn't safe for you to go off into the swamps alone. I can't let you do that."

"You can't stop me," Lou said and pushed off.

Chapter Eleven

Blood caked Zachary King's wrist and hands. It dripped from his fingers and trickled along the bottom of the canoe. He saw how bloody he was every time he glanced over his shoulder to see if he was making any headway. The answer was always the same. No.

For over two hours Zach had tried to free himself. He had tried to rub his wrists back and forth; he had attempted to twist them sideways. He had wrenched and tugged and pulled, all in vain. Mateo had done too thorough a job. There was no slack in the rope, no give, and the knots were iron tight.

It was now past three in the afternoon. In a stark, cloudless sky a scorching sun burned. Zach sweated constantly, profusely. His buckskins were drenched, his hair damp. He was exhausted, stiff, and sore. The only pleasant note in his unending ordeal was that his head didn't hurt quite as much as it had before, but it still hurt.

All this while, the canoe slowly drifted through the swamp. Which surprised Zach. He thought it would stay in the same spot, as would be the case in any body of still water. Drifting suggested a current, and since the drift was generally westward, in the direction of the Goujon estate and the Mississippi, he helped it along whenever the canoe encountered snags. Every time a log or downed limb or clump of submerged vegetation brought the canoe to a stop, he'd rock it until it was jarred loose.

At first, Zach had been encouraged by his slow but steady progress. Then it dawned on him that at the turtle's pace he was traveling, it would take the better part of a week to reach the plantation. He'd be long dead from dehydration, starvation, or predation, or perhaps a combination of all three.

Mateo had mentioned there were no alligators. But there were others predators, cougars and bears and other creatures—and one of them had been stalking the canoe for the past half an hour. Zach became aware of it when a twig snapped on a large, gloomy island he was passing, an island so thick with lush plant growth he couldn't peer more than a few yards into it.

Later, Zach heard furtive sounds, the pad of feet and soft splashing. Something was following him, of that there could be no doubt. Repeatedly he sought to catch sight of it by rising up and scanning the vicinity but never spotted it, although once he did see branches and leaves in a thicket move to the passage of a sizable animal.

Now Zach rose up again onto his elbows. The canoe was in a narrow channel hemmed in by high reeds, and he'd heard them rustle. Off to the left, reeds taller than he was were swaying and bending. Bending *toward* the channel, which told him that whatever was out there was coming toward him. He renewed his effort to slip his bounds, his wrists shrieking in protest as the rope seared deeper into his mutilated flesh.

A guttural cry, unlike any animal cry Zach had ever heard, confirmed the thing was getting nearer. The cry was sort of a cross between a coyote's yip and a boar's snort, yet different from both. Seconds later an awful odor assailed him, a reek so potent he held his breath in order not to breathe it in. The foul stench was similar to one he'd smelled once when he stumbled on a long-dead rotting deer swarming with maggots.

The canoe started to glide around a bend into more open water. Zach gave the reeds another scrutiny, then felt his pulse leap.

Something was staring at him. Dark, unblinking, malevolent eyes topped by beetling brows covered with hair were visible between parted reeds. Little else could be seen other than a vague outline, a squat, brutish, two-legged shape, likewise covered with dark brown or black hair.

Zach's skin crawled. The thing had to be the mysterious three-toed skunk ape mentioned by Jacques and Mateo. Neither had said whether there were any reports of it attacking people, but if it was the same creature that savaged Jacques's livestock, it was a predator, a meat eater, and like most predators it wouldn't allow an opportunity to feast go to waste.

The reeds swayed again and the creature was gone. It vanished so abruptly, it was as if the thing had blinked out of existence. For several seconds Zach wondered if he really had seen what he thought he saw or whether the heat and the loss of blood were having an effect. Another inhuman cry confirmed his senses were intact.

A rumbling, fierce snarl rent the humid air, a snarl of challenge tinged by primal rage. On its heels came a loud pounding, akin to fists on a chest. Then there ensued the rending and breaking of limbs and brush, punctuated by total, nerve-racking silence.

Zach didn't know what it all meant. Were the snarls a

```
***********************************
```
St. Helens Public Library
12/08/2021 2:37:15   503-397-4544
PM
```
***********************************
```

Title:	**The lonely men /**
Item ID:	34018000860785
Due:	12/29/2021

Title:
Ride the dark trail /
| Item ID: | 34018000860801 |
| Due: | 12/29/2021 |

Title:	**Blood truce /**
Item ID:	34018000816639
Due:	12/29/2021

Title:	**Blood kin /**
Item ID:	34018000816571
Due:	12/29/2021

*You saved $18.96 by using
the St. Helens Public Library today*

Account balance $0.00

WWW.CI.ST-
HELENS.OR.US/LIBRARY/

16 - 31

prelude to an attack or something else entirely? Most predators jumped their prey from ambush without any forewarning. The skunk ape, if that is indeed what it was, didn't seem to mind that Zach knew it was out there.

The open water was a blessing. Now the creature couldn't get at him without being seen, although with his arms and legs bound, whether Zach saw it or not was irrelevant. If the thing decided to kill him, he was helpless to prevent it.

The thought gave Zach added incentive to get free. He surged against the rope binding his wrists, refusing to let the agony deter him. Bunching his shoulder muscles, he strained with all his might. The anguish it provoked was almost unbearable. For the hundredth time he tried to move his wrists, and this time, wonder of wonders, he felt the rope give a little.

Zach persisted as the canoe sailed on. The hot sun burned him, insects buzzed his face, mosquitoes stopped to taste the blood still in his veins.

Up ahead was another channel through a densely wooded tract plunged in shadow. A loud splash to the rear whipped Zach's head around. Something had dived into the water near the reeds. He couldn't see what it was but its wake was obvious as it swam underwater on a parallel course with his and soon overtook the canoe. A dark form knifed powerfully by, stroking cleanly, ten yards out.

The skunk ape! Zach realized. And it was making for the wooded section through which he must pass. With renewed vigor he applied himself to the rope, virtually grinding it into his flesh as he rotated his wrists again and again.

The creature was almost to the patch of dry land. A dark head and shoulders heaved up out of the swamp. Then, in a few long bounds, it was in among the trees and weeds. It was astoundingly fast; all Zach glimpsed were long, crooked arms, stooped legs, and a hairy back.

Time was running out. Zach estimated he would reach the channel in another thirty to forty seconds. He rose onto his knees, still fighting the rope. It was loose but not quite loose enough.

Limbs were bobbing up and down due to weight pressed upon them. Leaves parted, and the same dark eyes below the same beetling brows glared out at him. A ferocious growl was borne on the breeze.

Zach's hands were soaking wet, and not from sweat. He wriggled them fiercely, up and down, side to side. Suddenly the rope slackened dramatically. A few sharp tugs and his right hand slipped free. Swinging his arms in front of him, he suffered enormous torment in both shoulders. His wrists were severely frayed, the flesh rubbed raw, but they weren't bleeding as badly as he had assumed.

Removing the rope and letting it drop, Zach snatched up the paddle. The canoe was a mere eight feet from the channel. He could swing around and go back the way he had come, but then he must find another waterway that would take him to the west. Anxiously scouring the trees, he decided to do the opposite. He dipped the paddle into the water and bent forward, stroking as fast as he could, first one side and then the other, propelling the canoe at top speed.

Zach's idea was to shoot through the channel before the skunk ape could stop him. Another growl heralded a rush of movement. Zach spotted it, angling in his direction, flying through the trees as a squirrel would do, leaping from limb to limb in death-defying hurdles. He pumped the paddle harder.

It wasn't good enough. The creature swept abreast of him, descended into the lower terrace, and dropped until it was only a few feet above Zach's head.

The channel, which was only three feet deep at that point, bore to the left. Forced to slow down, Zach took his eyes off the skunk ape so he could negotiate the bend safely.

With a great roar and the rending of small limbs, the abomination sailed out of the trees into the center of the channel. Water sprayed every which way. Immensely strong hands were thrust out to stop the canoe.

The terror of the swamp reared before Zach. Its stench was overpowering, but it was the horrid visage that chilled Zach to his marrow. Bestial features radiating ferocity were rendered all the more startling because they were also humanlike in aspect. Thin lips curled back over glistening fangs and the thing started to climb in by hooking a hairy three-toed foot over the side and surging upward.

Zach speared the paddle at the skunk ape's barrel chest but the monstrosity swatted it aside as if it were a twig. The thing had one leg in, one leg out. Latching its long fingers onto the canoe, it rose higher.

Never in Zach's life had he sorely wished he had a gun as much as he did at that moment. With his ankles bound he couldn't flee. He was stuck there, at the beast's mercy. Clearly, it meant to kill him. He stuck the paddle but the brute warded off the blow as casually as Zach would ward off a child's.

Without warning the canoe tilted at a steep angle. Zach grabbed hold to keep from being pitched into the water. He retained his grip on the paddle but nearly had it wrenched from his grasp when the skunk ape grabbed the other end and pulled.

Shrieking, the thing climbed all the way in. The addition of its bulk caused the canoe to rock and dip as if in a swell. Zach clung on, unable to defend himself. His loathsome adversary, though, had no need to grip the sides. Displaying uncanny balance, the creature stayed upright—and flung itself at him.

Louisa didn't like swamps. They were depressing places, damp and muddy and muggy, abounding with bugs and snakes, a domain fit for nightmares.

For hours Lou had been searching for her fiancé and all she had to show for it were bug bites and a cut on the back of her left hand where the tip of a sharp branch had scratched her. She was hungry. She was terribly thirsty. To slake both she periodically popped a piece of pemmican into her mouth and sucked on it until it was gone.

As much as Lou was reluctant to admit it, finding Zach would take a miracle. The swampland was seemingly limitless. Yet maybe, she mused, it was an illusion spawned by her inexperience. Maybe she had been traveling in circles all this time and wasn't far from where she had started.

No, that couldn't be, Lou reasoned. Like any frontiersman worthy of the name, she could mark her position by that of the sun. She had been bearing northward ever since she left the dock. So by rights she should be well into the swamp. Yet there had been no sign of another canoe, no sign of the man called Mateo or her beloved.

It didn't help matters that there were endless channels to navigate. The lowland was a maze where anyone who possessed less wilderness savvy than she did might easily wind up hopelessly lost.

Louisa was torn between a desire to forge on until hell froze over and the notion it might be wiser to return to the dock and wait for Mateo to show up. Then she'd make Mateo tell her where Zach was, and if any harm had befallen him, those responsible would suffer.

A wide pool appeared. Two herons rose into the air, their great wings flapping noisily. On a large log a turtle was basking, but it skittered into the water when the herons took flight.

Lou slanted toward yet another channel, her arms weary from so much paddling. The search had done her some good, though. She'd had a lot of time to think, particularly about her aunt and the others, and she had made up her mind about a number of things that wouldn't sit well with them.

For starters, Lou was heading back to the Rockies before the week was out. Zach and her would delay leaving only as long as it took to stock up on supplies. Lou realized Aunt Martha and her cousins had traveled a long way to see her and expected her to stick around for a month or so, as they originally planned, but she wanted nothing more to do with them.

They had brought it on themselves. Aunt Martha saying it was better if Zach were gone. Uncle Earnest's coldness. Uncle Thomas's outburst. Ethel's and Gladys's flightiness. Out of all of them, the only one Lou would miss would be Harry. Sincere, caring Harry.

Lou couldn't get over how gullible she'd been. She had really believed her relations had taken a shine to Zach and accepted him as one of their own. She thought she had Aunt Martha's fervent blessing, that Uncle Earnest and her cousins also approved. But their comments and conduct when Zach disappeared proved differently. They didn't think he was good enough for her. Aunt Martha had even come right out and told her it was for the best.

It crushed Lou to realize the only family she had was no family at all. By looking down their noses at Zach, by snubbing him, by treating him as the majority of whites did, they had severed whatever emotional ties formerly bound Lou to them.

Lou had had such high hopes, too. All the way across the prairie, day after day, week after week, she had daydreamed about how joyous their reunion would be. She'd imagined everyone would be happy for her. They would embrace Zach warmly and joyfully welcome him into the fold.

Lou should have known better. Aunt Martha never had been very fond of Indians, and Uncle Earnest had always been coldly remote. Her cousins Ethel and Gladys always treated her as if she didn't know enough to come in out of the rain without their help. Oh, they had all treated her decently enough, but there had always been an undercurrent of something she had been too young to put a name to. Now she could.

That name was prejudice.

Her father had known. One evening up in the high country, as they sat huddled by the fire on a blustery autumn eve, Lou had commented how much she missed everyone back home and asked her pa if he felt the same. It had surprised her when he took a while answering.

"I suppose I miss them a little. You've got to remember, princess, I was always the black sheep of our family. Nothing I've done ever suited them. They called me shiftless, saying all I ever do is chase dreams. They accused me of being reckless, of not being a good provider. I always want to know what's over the next horizon, and to them that's being short-sighted." Zeb had poked a stick at the fire. "There's no pleasing some folks, child, so don't even try. The best any of us can do is to please ourselves."

Lou hadn't quite understood what he meant at the time. Her father wasn't saying she should be selfish and think only of herself. He was instructing her to be true to her inner nature, to do as her conscience dictated, not as others wanted her to do.

An unusual sound from far off brought Lou's reverie to an end. She stopped paddling to listen. It sounded like a snarling painter, only different. Whatever made it was riled because it went on snarling and growling and carrying on something awful. Normally she would go out of her way to avoid such a beast but now she made for it on the off chance her fiancé was somehow involved.

In between strokes, Louisa loosened both pistols under her belt.

As the skunk ape sprang, Zach thrust the paddle at its abdomen. Exhibiting remarkable agility, the creature shifted, seized the other end, and ripped the paddle from Zach's hands. Raising it overhead, the ape threw it at him. Zach attempted to duck but he was too slow. The impact knocked him backward, and he heard the paddle fall into the channel.

Shrieking, the skunk ape pounced. Steely fingers wrapped around Zach's throat. Its fangs were poised to tear into his jugular, and in desperation Zach punched the monstrosity in the mouth.

The creature shrieked again, louder, then lifted Zach bodily into the air. He thought it would crush his neck or bite him, but instead the thing leaned closer, those dark eyes narrowing. It examined him, much as he had often examined small animals and insects he caught as a child. The brute sniffed several times, then a reddish tongue flicked out and the skunk ape licked his cheek.

All this Zach took in while he was being held two feet above the canoe, his bound legs dangling limp and useless. His breath was being choked off, and his lungs were in dire need of air.

For a moment the creature's eyes locked with his. In their simian depths lurked a raging, blazing hatred that defied all reason. The skunk ape opened its mouth again.

Instantly, Zach arced his fists up and in, boxing its ears, while slamming his knees into its groin. Yowling, the beast threw him over the side, into the water. Fortunately for Zach, his feet hit bottom first and he didn't go all the way under. With his ankles tied, he would be sorely taxed to regain the surface.

The skunk ape now had the canoe to itself. Roaring, it coiled to jump.

Zach rammed his shoulder against the canoe. It canted wildly, throwing the creature against the other side. Instead of falling overboard, though, the thing leaped straight up, into the overspreading branches of an ancient moss covered tree. As it leaped, its feet pushed against the canoe, sending it sailing off down the channel.

Now Zach had no means of escape. He hobbled to the bank and clambered out, dripping wet, dragging his legs. It was crucial he remove the other rope before the skunk ape closed in for the kill. Bending down, he pried at the slippery knot with his equally slippery fingers. Suddenly a shadow moved across him.

Zach glanced up. The creature was crouched on a limb

directly above. Its eyes were pits of hellfire, its gleaming teeth were bared. Pushing onto his knees, Zach cupped both hands together just as the living nightmare dropped from the branch. He swung, his knuckles clipping the thing across the shoulder, and bowled it over.

Screeching, the skunk ape toppled into the channel. Almost immediately it reared up out of the water, more incensed than ever, chattering and gibbering in a paroxysm of feral fury. A lithe bound brought it onto solid ground where it straightened and pounded its chest, working itself up to a feverish pitch.

Zach had been lucky so far but his luck wouldn't last forever. With his legs tied he was severely hampered. He couldn't run; he couldn't fight all that well. But he had to try. So long as breath remained in his body he would resist. Kings didn't give up. Nor did Shoshone warriors. To accept defeat without trying would dishonor his family and his tribe.

The abomination's temper tantrum ended. Hunched over, it moved slowly toward him, its fingers hooked like claws, saliva oozing over its lower lip and dribbling down its hairy chin.

Zach was no stranger to life-or-death struggles. At one time or another he had fought mountain lions, grizzlies, and hostiles. Yet never had he felt the creeping sense of dread that overcame him now. It wasn't fear. It was a deep-rooted instinct, as if the mere sight of the skunk ape struck some long-buried raw nerve from the dawn of time. He was scared, more than he had ever been scared before, but that didn't stop him from tucking his knees to chest and lashing out just as the skunk ape pounced.

The creature tried to sidestep but was hit in the side. It was staggered but it didn't go down. Wrapping one of its gargoyle hands around Zach's lower right leg, it steadied itself, then grinned fiendishly.

Zach tried to kick it again but missed. The ape, seizing both his legs, whipped them from side to side, flinging Zach back and forth. Caught like a leaf in a gale, Zach's shoulders absorbed most of the punishment. When the thing paused, Zach drove his feet up into its stomach. In retaliation the skunk ape beat and tore at his legs. Somehow, one of its fingers slid under the rope and became caught. When a tug failed to free it, the creature gripped the rope with its other hand and literally tore the rope off.

Taking advantage, Zach scrambled further up the bank and shoved upright. It was a mistake. The circulation in his feet had been cut off for too long. They wouldn't bear his weight. To his horror, he tottered wildly down the bank—toward the skunk ape.

The creature was sniffing the rope. Casting it aside, the beast growled hideously and spread its arms wide.

Zach sought to fling himself to the right but his traitorous feet betrayed him. Suddenly the monster had him in its grasp, in a bear hug. Their faces were inches apart. Its fetid breath, combined with the stench its body gave off, was enough to churn Zach's stomach. He fought to break loose but his strength was no match for the creature's.

Then the skunk ape did something truly devilish. It grinned. Its mouth curved in a humanlike smirk of triumph. The thing had him at its mercy, and they both knew it.

Zach had always known that one day he might die a violent death. Shoshone warriors learned to accept the fact and to go on with lives. But never in his wildest imaginings had he envisioned an end like this one—torn to pieces and possibly devoured by a hideous apparition that shouldn't exist.

The skunk ape tilted its head and opened its mouth wide to sink its teeth into Zach's neck.

"Let go of him, damn you!"

It was hard to say who was more surprised by the shout, Zach or the beast holding him. The skunk ape snarled and twisted toward the source, toward the channel, and over its shoulder Zach beheld the impossible. He thought it must be an illusion. He couldn't be seeing what he believed he saw—the woman he loved, in her buckskins, in a canoe, a Hawken pressed to her shoulder.

Louisa couldn't believe what she was seeing, either. The being that held her betrothed in its hairy grip was a demonic, obscene mockery all that was human, more beast than man yet manlike enough that if its head were shaved and it were fully clothed, it could walk down a city street without attracting undue notice.

The thing hadn't released Zach. Snarling, it took a step toward her.

"Let him go!" Lou repeated, doubting it could understand but hoping it would do so anyway and give her a clear shot.

Zach's initial shock passed and he found his voice. "Lou! Get out of here! Get away while you can!"

Lou would do no such thing, not with the one she loved in peril. She would save him or die trying. Slowly rising so as not to tip the canoe, she fixed a bead on the creature's left shoulder.

The skunk ape, rumbling like an enraged griz, glanced from Lou to Zach and back again, as if unsure which one it should kill first. Zach, in fear for Louisa's life, made a herculean effort to break its grip. He thrashed, he kicked, he bucked, but the iron bands around his torso were unaffected.

Lou raised her head from the rifle. Her sweetheart's struggles had her worried she might hit him by mistake. "Hold still!" she hollered.

Zach felt the creature tense. Guessing what it was about to do, he responded, "Lou! It's going to charge you!" And he was right. For suddenly the skunk ape flung him to the ground and bounded toward his fiancée.

The brute's rush was quick and silent. It crossed the intervening space in the blink of an eye, almost too fast for the eye to follow. But not faster than a bullet. Lou fired, rushing her shot, her Hawken spewing smoke and lead. The slug meant for the skunk ape's heart cored its lower ribs instead. Jolted backward, it clutched itself and screamed.

Zach rose to dash to Lou's aid. She was drawing one of her pistols.

The creature coiled but it didn't go after her. It leaped straight up, to the same low branch from which it had dropped onto Zach. For a heartbeat it paused, bestowing hate-filled glares on both of them. Then it vaulted to a higher limb, and to yet another, racing through the trees with astounding agility. Within moments it was gone, swallowed by the dank vegetation that had spawned it.

Louisa jumped to the bank. Zach met her and they embraced, clinging to one another in heartfelt relief. For a long time neither of them moved or spoke. It was Zach who eventually pulled back. Tenderly running a finger across her tear-drenched cheek, he said huskily, "I will love you forever."

They kissed, a kiss that fused their hearts and souls as well as their lips. A kiss that lasted as long as any kiss ever has or ever will.

Lou rested her head on his chest. "It's not over yet," she commented, wishing they could forgo what needed doing and head for the Rockies right that second.

"No, it's not," Zach grimly agreed. Those responsible were going to pay for what had been done to him. They were going to pay dearly.

Chapter Twelve

A sliver of moon hung over the Goujon estate, bathing the plantation in its silvery glow. The fields were quiet, the slaves having long since returned to their cabins for the night. The only sounds were Zach's and Lou's footfalls and the sighing of the breeze in the trees. They walked elbow to elbow, Lou with the rifle, Zach holding both pistols. They were a quarter of a mile from the mansion when they saw the tall figure in the middle of the trail, and he wasn't alone.

Racine wore the same flowing cloak he'd worn the night Zach and Adam Tyler chased him. In each hand he grasped two leashes, and at the end of each leash was a bristling mastiff. "I knew you would come," he said. "I have been waiting."

"Mateo is dead," Zach said.

The Cajun sighed. "I will miss him. He and I were like

brothers. He would do anything for me and I for him." One of the dogs strained against a leash and Racine pulled it back. "It was wrong of me to involve him."

Lou was incensed by his nonchalance. "That's not all that was wrong. You never should have agreed to my aunt's proposition." Zach had told her everything. "No woman is worth killing for."

"You think not?" Racine's cloaked flapped at a gust of wind. "Ask your fiancé if he would kill for you."

"I don't need to. I know Zach well enough to know he would kill to protect me, to defend me, yes. But he would never murder someone to win my hand." Lou had her trigger finger on the trigger.

"He would say he wouldn't but if it was the only way. . . ." Rancine shrugged. "We could debate morality all night. It would prove nothing. I want Gladys. I want her as I have never wanted anyone. And I will do whatever it takes to have her."

Lou remembered her aunt's remarks. "You're being played for a fool. My cousin doesn't even like you all that much. Aunt Martha is using you as a means to her end."

"You're just saying that to upset me."

"Am I? Since we met have you ever once heard me tell a lie?"

Racine's reply was slow in coming. "If what you say is true I will hold your aunt to account. But now—" he shook the leashes and the dogs whined and growled, eager to be released—"now I must finish what I started."

Zach nodded at the mastiffs. "I suppose you have an explanation all worked out in case anyone becomes suspicious."

"None is needed. Everyone is aware your fiancée went off looking for you earlier. They will think she found you, and the two of you were wandering about when you shouldn't have been."

"And the dogs just happened to find us?"

"A tragic oversight. They were not penned up at sunset

as they were supposed to be. Someone erred, and the two of you paid with your lives."

"You have it all thought out," Zach said.

The wily Cajun grinned. "I like to think so." His grin evaporated and he dropped the leashes. "Sic them! Kill them! Louis! Arnaud! Maslin! Verel! Kill! Kill! Kill!" Barking and snarling, the mastiffs obeyed, sweeping forward in a blinding rush, their massive bodies low to the ground.

Lou aimed at the foremost and fired. Her shot caught it in the chest, and the dog tumbled in a whirl of legs and tail. It came to a stop and was still, the rest veering to go around it.

Zach extended his right flintlock and squeezed off a shot. The slug ripped into the eyeball of another mastiff and the rear of its skull exploded in a spray of brains and gore. Dead on its feet, it still traveled several more yards before it collapsed. Zach was already extending the other pistol. The other two dogs were angling toward Lou, who was reloading the Hawken, her fingers flying. Zach centered the front bead on the lead dog's ear and brought it tumbling down.

That left one mastiff. Undeterred by the fate of its fellows, the dog coiled and sprang. Lou was just upending her powder horn over the Hawken's. She pivoted to the left but the mastiff rammed into her shoulder. The next moment she was on her back, the dog towering over her, her hands against its throat as she sought to prevent it from ripping open her own.

"Lou!" Zach darted to her side and beat at the dog's broad head with his pistols, to no effect. The mastiff completely ignored him, its slavering jaws sinking lower and lower, almost within reach of Lou's throat.

Dropping the left flintlock, Zach wrapped his arm around the dog's thick neck and attempted to pull it off. It was like trying to uproot a redwood. Zach smashed his remaining pistol across its skull but the dog never so much as yipped.

And now it's fangs were less than an inch from Lou. Dropping the other pistol, Zach looped his right arm around its neck, planted his moccasins, and heaved backward.

Lou saw what Zach was trying to do. She thrust upward with her knees, adding her strength to his. It wasn't enough to throw the mastiff off but the brute's body rose six or seven inches, enabling her to clutch at her waist. She fumbled with her Green River knife, nearly losing her grip as she yanked it from its beaded sheath.

The mastiff was snarling and snapping in a frenzy. A forepaw scraped Lou's arm, the claws tearing the sleeve and drawing blood.

For Zach, trying to hold onto the squirming, biting animal was like trying to wrestle a grizzly. The mastiff swung toward him, seeking to rip open his leg. He avoided a grinding gnash of razor teeth, then another bite, but it was only a question of time before those white fangs sank into his flesh.

Lou stopped trying to push the dog away. Securing her hold on the knife, she speared cold steel up into the dog's belly, not once, not twice, but three times in swift succession. Warm blood spattered her cheeks and forehead and trickled down her forearms.

At the third stab the mastiff uttered a strangled yip. It arched its spine, its great head lifting to the stars. A piercing howl split the night, a howl torn from the depths of its being. It lunged to the right and Zach let it go. Taking several stumbling strides, the dog sprawled onto the grass and lay trembling and whining. Mercifully, within half a minute it expired.

Zach helped Lou stand. Forgetting where they were, they hugged. Zach kissed her ear. "For a second there . . ." he said, leaving the horrible thought unspoken.

"I know," Lou said softly. If not for him, the dog would have slain her.

Remembering Racine, Zach spun. Their guns were empty, and given the manservant's expertise at French kickboxing, he might well overpower them and finish them off himself. But the Cajun wasn't there. For some inexplicable reason he had left during their clash with the mastiffs.

Lou wiped her knife blade clean on the last one, then hurriedly reclaimed the Hawken and resumed reloading. "Where do you reckon he got to?"

"We'll find out soon enough," Zach answered. The lights of the mansion gleamed beyond the tilled fields, twinkling like candles. He followed Lou's example and reloaded both of the pistols she had lent him. His own weapons, he assumed, had been stashed somewhere, perhaps in the stable since that was where Racine had jumped him. He'd hunt for them when his business at the mansion was over.

Dampness on her cheek reminded Lou of the spattered blood. She wiped her face with a sleeve. "It's just him against us," she remarked.

"Is it?" Zach said. "He might have more friends like Mateo waiting to ambush us. Then there's your aunt and the others."

"They won't do anything. Even Aunt Martha won't lift a finger against us."

"If you say so." Zach didn't share Lou's optimism. Any woman who would stoop to convincing someone else to commit murder for her was capable of anything. As he tamped black powder down a pistol barrel, he commented, "But I'm not turning my back to any of them. I wouldn't advise you to, either."

Presently they hiked on along the well-worn trail, side by side, their guns leveled. Zach glanced at Lou often, admiring her beauty, her courage. She was exactly the kind of woman he had always dreamed he'd marry: brave, loyal, and dependable. The courage and devotion she had shown in going into the swamp after him was remarkable.

Lou noticed him glancing at her and was going to chide him for not keeping his mind on what they were doing, but she didn't. He was forever staring at her when he thought she wouldn't see. Once she'd asked him why and he'd answered that her beauty was a magnet he couldn't resist. It was one of the sweetest things anyone ever said to her.

Lou thought of how Zach rushed to help when the mastiff pinned her on the ground, how he had tried to pull it off with his bare hands, and she grew all warm and tingly inside. She had another of her periodic urges to ravish him on the spot, but given the situation, she refrained.

At the mansion a rectangle of light flared at ground level, as it would if a door was opened and closed.

"Racine just went in," Lou said.

"I saw." Zach cocked both pistols. The stable loomed off to the right, the empty dog pens were to the left.

"I want you to leave Aunt Martha to me," Louisa requested.

Zach was scanning the lit windows for silhouettes but no one appeared to be looking out. "She tried to have me rubbed out. I take things like that sort of personal."

"I know. By rights you should deal with her. But she's my aunt, Stalking Coyote. I've known her since childhood. Please. For me."

When Lou used that tone Zach couldn't deny her anything. "Aunt Martha is yours. But Racine is mine and mine alone."

No voices were audible until Zach opened the rear door. He took the lead, gliding swiftly to the first junction. A maid was approaching, bearing a tray laden with long-stemmed wine glasses and a bottle. One look at Zach and Lou, with their guns and blood-stained buckskins, caused her to squeal in alarm, drop the tray, and bolt.

"Was it something we said?" Lou quipped.

The voices were a beacon, drawing them toward the parlor. Suddenly they heard a scream, then a wild shout, and a loud hubbub. Exchanging glances, they ran the rest of the way, slowing as they neared the doorway. Zach moved to the right jamb, Lou to the left.

Everyone was there: the three Goujons; Aunt Martha, Earnest and Harry; Uncle Thomas and his girls; even Adam

163

Tyler and George Milhouse. And one other. They were all on their feet except for Uncle Thomas, who was on the floor, blood seeping from his mouth. Gladys was in tears, with good reason. She was being hauled toward the door by Racine, who held a small pistol in his other hand.

Jacques Goujon was livid. "I repeat!" he thundered. "I demand to know the meaning of this outrageous conduct!"

"Demand all you want," the Cajun said flippantly. "All you need to know is that I am taking Mademoiselle Clark with me, and I will kill anyone who tries to stop me."

Auguste, smiling, moved forward. "Racine, *mon ami*. This is most unlike you. Let us talk this out like gentlemen."

Racine pointed the pistol at him. "Another step and you are a dead man." Auguste, bewildered, halted. "You call me your friend. Yet do you ever treat me like one? Like an equal? No, of course you do not. To you I am a servant, nothing more." Racine had slowed but he continued to slowly back toward the hall. "Yet that is of no consequence now. As of this moment I am a free man. I am taking my bride-to-be to where none of you will ever find us."

"Your bride-to-be?" Jacques sputtered. "What madness has come over you?"

Racine gazed at Gladys, who was weeping uncontrollably. "The madness of love. Since I set eyes on this woman I have adored her. And she responded in kind. She and I have done things I have done with no other. My heart is on fire for her, and I will have her at all costs." He glanced at Aunt Martha. "Our deal, Madame Livingston, is off."

"What deal, Racine?" This from Adam Tyler, who was over in a corner with Celeste.

It was the perfect moment. Zach entered, training the flintlocks on the Cajun's back. "I can answer that one." Racine started to pivot but Zach stopped him by declaring, "Try it and you're dead." Careful not to get within striking distance of the manservant's legs, Zach circled to the right until he could see Racine's face. "Now drop your pistol and kick it away."

Reluctantly, the Cajun complied.

Lou walked in. The shock that had silenced the rest at Zach's appearance was broken by questions and cries and exclamations as everyone tried to speak at once. Jacques Goujon hushed them by waving his arms and bawling for quiet. Then, gesturing at Lou and Zach, he pleaded, "Will one of you *please* tell us what is going on here?"

Lou did the honors. She kept it brief but she left nothing out. Stunned disbelief gripped most of them. No one interrupted. No one asked for more details. They'd heard enough. When Lou was done, the first to say something was Uncle Thomas, and it wasn't directed at her. Rising, he shook a finger at Martha.

"You promised him my *daughter?* How could you?"

Aunt Martha forced a laugh. "Really, Thomas. Don't throw a hissy fit. I'd never have let Racine have her. Gladys was the bait, is all."

Zach's disgust knew no bounds. "Shut up, both of you," he snapped. They both fell quiet, allowing Zach to turn his full attention to the Cajun. "Let go of the girl." When Racine hesitated, Zach pointed a pistol at his face. "Or die where you stand. Your choice."

Glaring pure spite, the Cajun released Gladys, and she immediately ran to her father, throwing herself into his arms.

Zach wasn't done. "Lou, slide your knife across the floor to him."

"Just shoot the bastard," Louisa responded.

"He's mine, remember?" Zach reminded her. "I'll do it my way."

Lou didn't like it. She didn't like it one bit. But she did as he requested, shoving her Green River knife to within a few inches of the Cajun's shoes.

Jacques Goujon cleared his throat. "Monsieur King, am

I to understand you are challenging Racine to a knife duel? Here and now?"

"Something like that." Zach glanced at Auguste. "In that trophy room you showed me yesterday I saw a cabinet with rifles and pistols and knives. Isn't one of those knives a bowie?"

"Oui."

"Will you be so kind as to fetch it for me?" Zach asked. "I need to borrow it for a few minutes. Racine took mine."

Auguste looked at his father, who nodded, and the son ran out of the room.

Racine was surprisingly calm given the circumstances. "Your own bowie and other weapons are hidden in the loft in the stable." He nudged the Green River knife with a toe. "As for this toy, I do not need it to defeat you. I can best you with my hands and feet alone."

"You can try," Zach said.

George Milhouse tittered and sat back down, propping his feet on a mahogany table and setting his cane across his lap. "This should be plumb entertainin', " the old trapper remarked. "We might as well make ourselves comfortable."

Earnest Livingston sneered at him. "You find violence amusing?"

The mountaineer chuckled. "It must be all those books."

"I beg your pardon?"

"You're a lawyer, aren't you? You spend so much time with your head buried in law books, you never see what the real world is like. Violence is the natural order of things, city man. Take a walk in the woods sometime. You'll see birds eatin' bugs, snakes and bobcats eatin' birds, painters eatin' deer, and grizzlies eatin' everything under the sun. Violence, everywhere you look."

"They do that to eat," Earnest said archly.

"Killin' is still violence, whether it's done to fill your belly or otherwise."

Celeste Goujon came toward the middle of the parlor,

Adam at her side. "Racine," she said softly, "I can't tell you how disappointed I am. We have always regarded you as one of the family."

"With all due respect, mademoiselle," the Cajun said, "you have regarded me no differently than you regarded your pet mastiffs. You are, to be blunt, a snob. You and your whole family."

Adam Tyler's right arm rose but stopped midway. "Apologize for your insult."

"I regret that I cannot."

"Then honor demands I formally challenge you to a duel on Bloody Island. Provided you survive the knife fight, of course."

"Of course."

Lou was perplexed at how casually Tyler made the challenge and how readily Racine accepted it. She was under the impression they were fairly good friends.

Celeste had turned to the gambler. "You would fight and possibly die for the sake of my honor?"

"I would do anything for you," Adam frankly admitted.

They clasped hands, a tender interlude shattered by the arrival of Auguste, who was out of breath but bearing a bowie in a black leather sheath. "Here it is, Monsieur King," he huffed, handing it over.

Zach accepted the knife and motioned for Auguste to move over against the wall. Beckoning Lou, he gave her both pistols and she tucked them under her belt. For a few moments their eyes locked, expressing more than they ever possibly could with words. "Be careful," Lou whispered.

Hefting the bowie to test its balance, Zach moved around in front of Racine. The knife was exquisite. It sported a black walnut hilt, a polished brass guard, and a superbly crafted blade slightly different from most of the bowies he had seen in that blade was double-edged along the length of the curve to the tip. It felt as if it were part of him, molding to his hand better than his own.

Racine bent and picked up the Green River knife. He

167

twirled it on his fingertips, then flipped it high into the air and deftly caught it by the hilt. "You would be well advised, Monsieur King, to change your mind. I am not without skill with edged weapons." He executed a series of lightning slashes, reversed his grip, and held the knife down low, close to his waist. Adopting a wide, T-shaped stance, he sidled forward.

Zach was motionless, the bowie at his side, the hilt held so that his thumb was along the top edge of the grip.

"Whenever you are ready," Racine said. When Zach neither replied nor moved, he flashed the Green River knife in a dazzling figure-eight pattern, whether to intimidate Zach or to loosen up his sinews, Zach couldn't say. "What are you waiting for, monsieur?"

"You're in an awful hurry to die," Zach said.

"I could say the same about you." Racine attacked, sweeping his right leg in a groin kick while at the selfsame instant he cleaved the Green River knife at Zach's head. It was a lethal combination, going low and high at the same time.

Zach waited until the last possible split second, until it was too late for the tall Cajun to check the swing or the kick. Leaping backward, Zach whipped the bowie in an arc. Steel glittered in the glow of the chandelier, flashing true.

Some of the women gasped.

Jacques Goujon declared, "*Mon Dieu!*"

Racine was ramrod straight, staring in stupefied wonder at the black walnut hilt protruding from his chest. The Green River knife clattered to the floor. Placing his hands on the bowie, Racine gripped it, as if to pull it out. Scarlet spurted from his mouth and nose and he swayed. Taking a faltering step toward Zach, he blurted, "This cannot be."

"Practice," Zach responded. "Hours and hours of practice."

More scarlet gushed as Racine bowed every so slightly, then swiveled toward Gladys. "You pledged you would be mine always," he said without bitterness and died, folding in upon himself and sprawling onto his side.

Zach went over, propped a moccasin against the Cajun's hip, and wrenched the bowie out. Wiping it on Racine's jacket, he offered it to Jacques Goujon. "Thank you for the use of your weapon."

"You may keep it, Monsieur King," Jacques said. "Every time I look at it, I would be reminded of my manservant."

"I have nothing of value to offer you in return," Zach said.

"Consider it a gift."

Louisa lowered the Hawken. They were almost done. There was only one thing left to do, and it was up to her to do it. She moved toward her aunt, handing the rifle to Zach as she passed him.

Aunt Martha was gawking at the Cajun like most everyone else. Blinking, she grinned feebly and said, "Now, now, little one. I know what you're thinking. But you shouldn't hold it against me. I had your best interests at heart."

Molten fire pulsed through Louisa's veins. She wasn't aware she had clenched her fists until she felt her nails digging into her palms. "I'm an adult now, Aunt Martha. I make my own decisions. What you did was despicable."

"But you'll forgive me, right? My sweet little Lou?"

"Wrong," Lou said and hit her aunt flush on the jaw. Her hand and wrist lanced with pain, but it was worth it to see Aunt Martha teeter back against a chair and fall, taking the chair down with her.

Uncle Earnest angrily moved toward her, declaring, "How dare you!" He drew up short at a distinct metallic click.

Zach had aimed the Hawken at him.

Lou bent over her shocked aunt. "Do you have any idea what you've done? Do you know how much I looked forward to our reunion? How happy it made me to see all of you again?" Tears tried to well up but Lou wouldn't let them. "I loved you. I loved all of you. And I thought you loved me."

"We do," Aunt Martha said.

"You don't know the meaning of the word!" Lou practically screeched. She cocked her fist to strike her aunt again, then jerked her arm down. Shaking from the intensity of the emotions roiling within, Lou took a few deep breaths.

"Forget about her, Louisa," Uncle Thomas interjected. "Come back to Ohio with the girls and me."

"I never want to see any of you again. From this day on my ties with the Livingstons and Clarks are cut. The Kings are my family now. Zach and I are going back to the mountains to live out our lives. Try to stop us and you will regret it." Lou headed toward Zach, pausing when she saw Harry, who was about to cry himself.

"I had no part in it, Louisa. Honest."

"I know. What I just said doesn't apply to you." Lou touched his cheek. "You're the only one who truly cares for me, the truest friend of all. Write me from time to time, will you? I'll do the same."

Zach wanted her out of there, wanted her turmoil to end. "It's time we were leaving," he announced. Lou, nodding, joined him, and he put his arm around her. En route to the door he said to Adam Tyler, "If it's all right with you, we'll collect our things and spend the night at your place. In a day or two we'll head for the Rockies and be out of your hair."

"You're welcome to stay as long as you like," the gambler said.

Louisa gazed over her shoulder at the people she had once cherished almost as much as her own father and mother. She sniffled, then squared her shoulders and let Zach guide her out. Her relatives were the past. He was the future. Together, they would forge a whole new life for themselves. She should be happy, not sad.

The best was yet to come.

WILDERNESS DOUBLE EDITION

SAVE $$$!

Savage Rendezvous by David Thompson. In 1828, the Rocky Mountains are an immense, unsettled region through which few white men dare travel. Only courageous mountain men like Nathaniel King are willing to risk the unknown dangers for the freedom the wilderness offers. But while attending a rendezvous of trappers and fur traders, King's freedom is threatened when he is accused of murdering several men for their money. With the help of his friend Shakespeare McNair, Nate has to prove his innocence. For he has not cast off the fetters of society to spend the rest of his life behind bars.

And in the same action-packed volume...

Blood Fury by David Thompson. On a hunting trip, young Nathaniel King stumbles onto a disgraced Crow Indian. Attempting to regain his honor, Sitting Bear places himself and his family in great peril, for a war party of hostile Utes threatens to kill them all. When the savages wound Sitting Bear and kidnap his wife and daughter, Nathaniel has to rescue them or watch them perish. But despite his skill in tricking unfriendly Indians, King may have met an enemy he cannot outsmart.

_4208-8 $4.99 US/$5.99 CAN

WILDERNESS

#24

Mountain Madness

<=======================>

David Thompson

When Nate King comes upon a pair of green would-be trappers from New York, he is only too glad to risk his life to save them from a Piegan war party. It is only after he takes them into his own cabin that he realizes they will repay his kindness...with betrayal. When the backshooters reveal their true colors, Nate knows he is in for a brutal battle—with the lives of his family hanging in the balance.

___4399-8 $3.99 US/$4.99 CAN

Dorchester Publishing Co., Inc.
P.O. Box 6640
Wayne, PA 19087-8640

Please add $1.75 for shipping and handling for the first book and $.50 for each book thereafter. NY, NYC, and PA residents, please add appropriate sales tax. No cash, stamps, or C.O.D.s. All orders shipped within 6 weeks via postal service book rate. Canadian orders require $2.00 extra postage and must be paid in U.S. dollars through a U.S. banking facility.

Name_____
Address_____
City_____State_____Zip_____
I have enclosed $_____ in payment for the checked book(s).
Payment <u>must</u> accompany all orders. ❑ Please send a free catalog.
       CHECK OUT OUR WEBSITE! www.dorchesterpub.com

WILDERNESS

#25
FRONTIER MAYHEM

←——————————————————————→

David Thompson

The unforgiving wilderness of the Rocky Mountains forces a boy to grow up fast, so Nate King taught his son, Zach, how to survive the constant hazards and hardships—and he taught him well. With an Indian war party on the prowl and a marauding grizzly on the loose, young Zach is about to face the test of his life, with no room for failure. But there is one danger Nate hasn't prepared Zach for—a beautiful girl with blue eyes.

___4433-1 $3.99 US/$4.99 CAN

Dorchester Publishing Co., Inc.
P.O. Box 6640
Wayne, PA 19087-8640

Please add $1.75 for shipping and handling for the first book and $.50 for each book thereafter. NY, NYC, and PA residents, please add appropriate sales tax. No cash, stamps, or C.O.D.s. All orders shipped within 6 weeks via postal service book rate. Canadian orders require $2.00 extra postage and must be paid in U.S. dollars through a U.S. banking facility.

Name_____
Address_____
City_____ State_____ Zip_____
I have enclosed $_____ in payment for the checked book(s).
Payment <u>must</u> accompany all orders. ❑ Please send a free catalog.
      CHECK OUT OUR WEBSITE! www.dorchesterpub.com

WILDERNESS

BLOOD FEUD

←————————————→

David Thompson

The brutal wilderness of the Rocky Mountains can be deadly to those unaccustomed to its dangers. So when a clan of travelers from the hill country back East arrive at Nate King's part of the mountain, Nate is more than willing to lend a hand and show them some hospitality. He has no way of knowing that this clan is used to fighting—and killing—for what they want. And they want Nate's land for their own!

___4477-3 $3.99 US/$4.99 CAN